BRIDE'S DILEMMA

It was love at first sight for Tina when she saw John Trecarrel, a cynical, world-weary widower, years older than herself. Before she realised what was happening he had married her and borne her out to his home in the romantic Caribbean. And then, having married in haste, Tina had plenty of time to repent at leisure when she found she not only had to compete with the memory of John's beautiful first wife, Joanna, but with the even more alarming presence of Joanna's equally beautiful cousin Paula.

BRIDE'S DILEMMA

Violet Winspear

ATLANTIC LARGE PRINT
Chivers Press
and
John Curley & Associates Inc.

Library of Congress Cataloging in Publication Data

Winspear, Violet.
Bride's dilemma.

Originally published: London: Mills & Boon, 1966.
(Atlantic large print.)
1. Large type books. I. Title.
[PR6073.I5543B7 1982] 823'.914 81–19503
ISBN 0–89340–440–3 (J. Curley) AACR2

British Library Cataloguing in Publication Data

Winspear, Violet
Bride's dilemma.—Large print ed.—
(Atlantic large print)
I. Title
823'914[F] PR6073.I553/
ISBN 0–85119–461–3

This Large Print edition is published by Chivers Press, England, and John Curley & Associates, Inc, U.S.A. 1982

Published by arrangement with Mills & Boon Limited

U.K. Hardback ISBN 0 85119 461 3
U.S.A. Softback ISBN 0 89340 440 3

BRIDE'S DILEMMA

All the characters in this book have no existence outside the imagination of the Author, and have no relation whatsoever to anyone bearing the same name or names. They are not even distantly inspired by any individual known or unknown to the Author, and all the incidents are pure invention.

CHAPTER ONE

CHORLEY-ON-SEA in March, with the wind lashing the sea into white caps, and gulls mewing in a rather lonely way above the headland where in the holiday season families brought picnic hampers and lazed in the sun-warmed heather.

Now the place was desolate, cut off from gaiety, restored to the stark beauty Tina Manson liked.

She stood on the headland, a slender young thing in a blue suede jacket over a sweater and tapering trews, braced against the wind which tangled her fine ashen hair and whipped colour into cheeks that were pale from the long hours she spent typing in the rather stuffy office of a local firm of solicitors. Today was Sunday, however, and for a while Tina was free to enjoy all this, thoughts of work, Aunt Maud, that dreary old house on Dulcey Avenue pushed to the back of her mind.

She had a bar of chocolate in her pocket and she was reaching for it when someone said: 'Please, don't move just yet. Stand just as you are, gazing out towards the sea as though the realization of a dream awaits you on the other side of the horizon.'

Tina instinctively obeyed the request, while her pulses gave a jolt of surprise that mingled with quick interest. Never before had she heard such a compelling male voice, but she knew that voices could disappoint you. Over the phone at the office they often sounded far more interesting than their owners turned out to be. The wind wrapped a pale coil of hair about her slim neck, but she refrained from moving it, though it tickled a bit, for she had guessed that she was being sketched.

Artists did drift into Chorley now and again, bringing their easels with them. The coastline had its attractions, a rugged arm embracing a town that peered out into a dullness that sent many of its young people to London for a livelihood.

'That's got it,' the man said. 'Now you can relax.'

Tina, on the contrary, went rather tense. It wasn't in her nature to start casual conversations with strangers, and she knew he had come suddenly closer to her, taking a long stride through the heather. She turned with swift, unaware grace and took him in with her wood-smoke eyes. He was tall, lean, tanned by a sun that had never shone over England. Thick hair flecked with grey moved in the wind above the face of a man who had seen much, travelled far, and picked up along the way an experience that had left him with a sad and cynical mouth. These impressions ran swiftly through Tina's mind, like a stream in spate picking up scattered leaves, then he smiled and grew strangely younger as lines fanned out beside eyes as blue as the sea—not the sea here at Chorley, but the sea as Tina imagined it could be far over the horizon.

'Caricatures are a hobby of mine. Here, take a look at yourself as seen through the eyes of someone else, for mirrors can lie and words have for each of us only the meaning we wish to read into them.'

Tina took the sketching block he held out to her, and she saw that in light, sure strokes he had captured her air of loneliness on this headland under drifting clouds. Her legs in her slender trews seemed to want to dart far away, her loosened hair played about a profile that was fine-boned, and stamped with wistfulness.

With a diffident little laugh she met the stranger's eyes. 'I'm grateful you've been kinder than caricaturists usually are to their victims,' she said.

'I'm rarely cruel to young things and animals,' he drawled, pushing the block into a capacious pocket of his tweed jacket and taking out a briar pipe from the other one. 'I'm sorry I can't offer you a cigarette,' he added, the stem of the briar jutting from a corner of his mouth as he patted his pockets for matches.

'I don't smoke.' Tina, who was twenty-one, was glad he hadn't taken her for a complete kid despite her lack of make-up and the knockabout clothes she was wearing. She watched him feed the flame of a match to the tobacco in his pipe, a long-fingered hand shielding it, a tousle of grey-flecked hair meeting his right eyebrow. Strong smoke sailed to her nostrils and she wondered what this lean, sophisticated stranger was doing in Chorley of all places.

He seemed to read the question in her mind, for he said. 'I've been visiting friends farther along the coast. My car broke down here last night and I'm putting up at the Tudor Arms while it's undergoing repairs.'

'Chorley must seem pretty dull to you?' Tina took a bite at her milk-flake and knew he was regarding her with twin glints of amusement in those sea-blue eyes.

'You find it dull yourself, don't you,

child?' he parried.

'I suppose you've got me tabulated as a backwoods girl dreaming of going to the big city in search of fame as a model or a TV star,' she said, crossing swords with him, albeit with more defiance than skill.

'When a girl stands gazing out to sea with wistfulness etched in every line of her, then I'd say she was scanning the horizon for something new. A dream, maybe . . . an adventure.' He narrowed his eyes against the updrifting smoke of his pipe. 'When I was a boy, down in Cornwall, I used to watch the sea and dream of sailing to its farthest shores.'

She looked at him and knew he had made his dreams come true, but one dream of his had floundered on rocks and he still carried the wounds—they etched his lean face in lines that made it difficult to assess his age. The grey in his hair was nothing to go by, for Tina could never remember a time when Aunt Maud had been other than grey, and Tina had lived with her aunt for almost twenty years. Maybe he was forty. Anyway, he was rather nice to talk to. He wasn't just picking her up, leading her on, amusing himself for half an hour with a shy country girl.

'I would like to travel,' she admitted, 'but there isn't much hope of my doing more than dream about it.'

'Nonsense!' He threw her words to the wind with a gesture that blew sparks out of the bowl of his pipe. 'We live in an age when the doors of most of the world are open to everyone with a dash of initiative in them. You could travel abroad with a group of girl friends and do it quite cheaply—if that's the drawback. Is it? Or have you a pair of stuffy parents who keep you on leading strings?'

The moment he said this, there spiralled through Tina an urge to confide in him, but confidences established a link and she hesitated to weld one between herself and this disturbing stranger. When they parted, she knew he would return to a life that was totally different from her own, the memory of their conversation drifting away from him like his pipe smoke. But she would not forget so easily. It might hurt—a lot—to have to remember that here on this lonely headland she had opened her heart to a man with sea-blue eyes, and a dent in his chin that made her fingertips tingle to explore it.

She was faintly shocked, deep down inside herself, by such thoughts about a man. She had always found those in Chorley quite uninteresting—which was just as well, for Aunt Maud had never encouraged her to take an interest in them.

'My parents are dead,' she said, hands in the pockets of her trews, her gaze following the graceful swoop of a gull on to something finned in the sea. 'I lost them when I was about two, and my father's unmarried sister took me in. I—I suppose you could call Aunt Maud a bit of a Victorian. What I mean is . . .'

'I can guess,' put in that vibrant voice, with something about it that was not quite English, though he had said he came originally from Cornwall.

Tina looked at him. Her stance was boyish, independent. She wasn't asking for pity.

There was no pity in his eyes, only the understanding of a man of wide experience. 'Your aunt has never been wanted by a man, and it's a cruelty she has never forgiven—anyone,' he said quietly.

He had cut straight to the heart of the matter and she liked him, very much, for not being amused by the classic situation of an orphaned girl tied by a sense of duty to a cold-hearted guardian. She knew, none better, that her loyalty to Aunt Maud was unappreciated and taken for granted, but she couldn't bring herself to walk out on someone elderly and friendless.

'It would be wrong to deny yourself a wider horizon if this aunt of yours cared for you,' said this dangerously perceptive stranger who had walked into her life, and who would in a while walk out of it. 'It isn't enough to come up here and dream for an hour. At least try and manage a holiday abroad, or are foreigners in Auntie's opinion not to be trusted?'

When Tina smiled and shrugged her slim shoulders, his quizzical eyes probed the sensitive angles of her face. 'Exactly how old are you?' he asked, evidently of the opinion that she was young enough not to mind telling him.

She told him.

'What happens when you want to get married? I presume it's on your agenda?'

'Only as a footnote.' She grinned and her small, pale face took on a triangular charm. 'Look, isn't this a rather peculiar conversation for a couple of strangers to be having? I'm sure you can't really be interested in my problems.'

'It's a little like a scene out of a book,

isn't it?' His jutting briar sent up spirals of smoke, his navy-blue silk-knit tie fluttered out of his jacket, his air of easy assurance spoke of money and a knowledge of women. 'We're talking like this because we're passing ships in the afternoon, because I picked up your distress signal and I'm an older tug who might be able to help you navigate a sticky patch. You're bogged down in it, aren't you, child? You're going to have to pull out before you grow into a joyless facsimile of this aunt of yours. It could happen—it will, if you let it.'

Tina shivered, chilled by the inevitable as clouds scurried low overhead and turned the sea as sombre as her future on Dulcey Avenue, hemmed in by dark-papered walls and her aunt's inhibitions. Yes, she wanted to pull out while she was still young and hopeful, but her aunt wasn't a robust woman. Right now she was in hospital, awaiting the result of tests which might indicate an operation.

Aunt Maud hadn't liked the idea of going into hospital, but her doctor had been insistent. Tina still felt hurt by the scene there had been, for her aunt had got it into her head that her niece didn't wish to nurse her. 'You're selfish, like that mother of yours!' she had stormed. 'Pleasure outings, that's all she thought about—'

Tina's parents had been killed in a coach crash and it was an old cry of Aunt Maud's that Tina took after her mother. She had been very much younger than George Manson when they had married and much too pretty for his sister's liking . . .

'I must be getting home.' Tina swung away from the grumbling grey sea. 'It looks as though it's going to rain.'

They walked side by side through the wind-tossed heather, she and this long-legged stranger, and he talked about the West Indies, where he lived, describing in vivid detail an island called Ste. Monique. But all too soon they had reached the market square, and a flurry of raindrops dewed the determined brightness of Tina's smile when they paused outside the black and white timbered inn where he was putting up. It had been fleeting but memorable, this meeting!

'I've enjoyed talking to you,' she smiled. 'If I never see Ste. Monique I shall always know a little what it looks like.'

'I've enjoyed our conversation as well . . . little girl lost.' He took her slender hand into his strong-fingered one and gazed straight down into her eyes. 'Remember what I said to you up on the headland, you have a life of your own to lead. Don't waste it. Youth is such a short and precious time.'

He gave the words a deep, personal meaning, while the lines beside his mouth seemed deeper engraved.

Impulsively she said: 'May I know your name?'

He broke into a smile. 'Will you forget me if you have no proper label to hang on me?'

She brushed a strand of hair from her eyes and shook her head. 'It's just that I seem to know your face—'

'I'm John Trecarrel,' he told her quietly.

The name slipped into her mind and in a flash connected itself to a selection of remarkable bronzes recently shown in a magazine. One of those stiff, studio photographs of the sculptor had accompanied the bronzes. 'You're John Trecarrel the sculptor!' she exclaimed, not in awe but in a kind of warm satisfaction.

His lips quirked into a grin and she saw a hint of raffishness in him, glimpsed the man he had been at her age. 'Are you going to tell me your name?' he asked. 'Or must I just remember you as the girl on the cliff?'

She told him her name, pleased he had asked for it.

'Good-bye, Tina!' His fingers pressed hers, then she walked across the market square without looking back. She didn't have to. His lean, dark face and long-limbed frame were etched on her mind.

* * *

While Tina's aunt was in hospital she was staying with the people next door, a nice, easy-going family. Kitty, the daughter, was a lively young person with several boy-friends, and very naturally she was of the opinion that Tina should get out and about a bit more. 'You tie yourself hand and foot to that nagging old aunt of yours,' she said with youthful candour. 'An occasional movie is about your limit. Look, come to our club dance on Friday and I'll get you fixed up with a nice boy.'

'Thanks for the offer, Kitty,' Tina smiled, 'but I can't leave Aunt Maud without a visitor on Friday.'

'You can come along to the club after you've been in to see her,' Kitty pointed out.

'I-I'll see,' Tina said, but she knew she wouldn't go to the club. She lacked the sparkle that appealed to young men and was never at her best with them. The slick repartee they expected from a girl was not her kind of language.

Each evening Tina visited her aunt, taking in the fresh fruit which Kitty's father purchased for her at the market garden where he worked. A good deal of it remained untouched on her aunt's locker, but when Tina suggested that the woman in the next bed might enjoy some of it, Aunt Maud sourly rejoined that the woman had relatives of her own so let them supply her with fruit.

It was on the Friday evening that the doctor in charge of Maud Manson's case had a talk with Tina. An operation must be performed, but Miss Manson's heart was strong and he had every confidence in a successful result. He patted Tina's shoulder and told her not to worry, but Aunt Maud was no longer a young woman and it was natural that Tina should be concerned.

She didn't have to work on Saturdays, and the following morning she busied herself in her own house, her hair swathed in a scarf as she wielded her aunt's heavy vacuum-cleaner. The rooms were stuffed with dark furniture which had belonged to Aunt Maud's parents, and as Tina worked away she thought of Kitty next door and the way she had come in from the dance last night, lipstick on her chin and a turbulent pink in her cheeks. It must make life much easier if you were able to face it in such a carefree manner, Tina reflected, recalling the way Kitty had danced her flounced petticoat round the bedroom and announced that she was thinking of falling in love with her latest boy-friend.

'I didn't know a girl had to *think* about falling in love,' Tina had laughed.

'You are an innocent, Tina,' Kitty had scoffed. 'Of course a girl must think about it. Only a goof would let herself go crumbly at the knees over *anything*.' Then, perched on the foot of her bed and rolling off her tights, she had asked: 'Ever liked someone special?'

Tina had shaken her head, remembering all the time a pair of sea-blue eyes and a deep voice saying: 'Good-bye, Tina!'

Her housework finished, she finally settled down in the kitchen with a cup of coffee. The radio was on and a record was playing when a loud rat-tat sounded on the front door, jerking Tina's heart into her throat. She was thinking worriedly of Aunt Maud as she skimmed up the passage to open the door—a stout, red-faced man and a fur-coated woman stood on the step. They were total strangers to Tina—and yet there was something vaguely familiar about the woman's face.

'You must be young Tina.' The woman took her in from her scarf-swathed hair to her flatties. 'We're your Aunt Sarah and Uncle Sidney.'

Sarah Hutton! Aunt Maud's sister, who had married a publican years ago and gone to Birmingham to live!

'Here, you look bowled over to see us,' the woman said. 'Didn't Maudie tell you she'd written to me?'

Tina shook a bewildered head. Aunt Maud and her sister had quarrelled a long time ago, when Sarah had learned at their father's funeral that he had left this house and its furniture to Maud. This was Sarah's first visit in Tina's experience—and gazing wide-eyed at the brash, big-boned woman, she decided that she didn't much like the look of her.

'Well, aren't you going to invite us in?' Sarah demanded.

'O-of course.' Tina stood aside for them.

Sidney Hutton brushed against her, and when she drew back he leered at her, evidently the type who considered himself irresistible!

'This house hasn't changed a bit, Sid,' Sarah Hutton threw back over her shoulder. 'That's still the same varnished paper on the wall—and, good grief, Maud's kept that old dresser, and every willow-pattern plate and cup is still intact!'

She laughed aloud and swung round, taking in every aspect of the sitting-room.

'Would you like some coffee?' Tina asked. 'It won't take me long to make it.'

'We've had a drink at the Tudor Arms, where we're staying for the week-end.' The woman slipped out of her fur coat, while her husband held his cigar like a gun and looked round with insolent eyes for an ashtray.

'I-I'll get you a saucer, Mr. Hutton.' Tina darted into the kitchen, where she flipped off her scarf and apron. She was flustered by this totally unexpected visit, and for some reason she couldn't believe that Aunt Maud's sister had travelled down from Birmingham out of sincere concern and anxiety. If you were anxious about someone, you asked right away how they were, you didn't take more interest in their house. Tina felt a current of anger shoot through her when she returned to the sitting-room to hear Sarah Hutton remarking to her husband that Maud had kept this house in good repair and that with the property market on the boom, the place was worth three times its original price.

Sidney Hutton was now sprawled in a fireside chair, his legs across the hearthrug, and as Tina placed a saucer on the arm of his chair he flicked a look over her that made her itch to slap his face. 'Thanks, Tina,' he smiled. 'So you're George's little girl, eh? All grown up and keeping house while your auntie's ill?'

'Poor old Maudie!' Sarah sat down and took a cigarette-case out of her big alligator bag. 'I was quite cut up when I got her letter. It's true we haven't seen each other for a long time, but family differences have to be forgotten at a time like this. She said she's got to have an operation. Is that right, Tina?'

'Yes, Mrs. Hutton.' Tina went and sat at the other side of the table to avoid Sidney Hutton's appraisal. Beastly man! His eyes felt like beetles running over her.

His wife puffed out cigarette smoke.

'We'd like to go in and see her this afternoon, Tina. I don't suppose you'll mind giving up your visiting hour?'

'Of course not, Mrs. Hutton, as you've come all this way. I'm sure Aunt Maud will be pleased to see you. You'll have lots to talk about.'

As if suspecting a tinge of irony in Tina's tone, Sarah narrowed her eyes. Then, seeing only a slim, pale-haired girl with a fragile pitch to her cheekbones and a mouth that was all heart, the woman complacently crossed her alligator shoes and flicked ash with a heavily ringed hand. 'So Maudie didn't tell you she'd written to me? She was always a bit secretive.' Then Sarah leant forward, a smile curling on her large, painted mouth. 'I bet you find her a bit of a trial to live with, don't you?'

'I'm used to Aunt Maud,' Tina said loyally. 'She's brought me up—I owe her a lot.'

'All the same, she can't be none too lively for a bit of a kid to live with. I bet she hasn't changed much. Here, Sid,' Sarah swivelled to look at him, 'd'you remember that time she caught us cuddling in the parlour with the lights out? I knew she told Father a nice old tale, and I always say that's why he left everything to her. Chaste because she was never chased, that's Maudie. Still, I don't like to think of her lying ill in hospital. I mean, she's getting on. She's older than George was.'

Sarah stared at Tina through her cigarette smoke as though searching for a likeness to her brother. 'What do you work at, Tina?' she asked. 'Do you wait on tables in one of the tea-rooms?'

'I'm a typist in an office,' Tina replied, her fingers in a knot in her lap. She was hurt that Aunt Maud hadn't mentioned writing to her sister. Hurt and mystified.

Then she gave a start as she realized that Sidney Hutton was speaking to her. He wanted to know if she was courting and she saw him grin to himself when she shook her head.

'Chorley never had many prizes to offer when I was a girl,' his wife put in. 'I don't suppose the situation has changed much. Now up in Birmingham you'd notice the difference, Tina. We run a smart roadhouse and we could offer you quite a nice little job, you know, helping with the lunchtime trade and doing some counter work in the evenings. We get some smart chaps in. Nearly all of them run their own cars.'

'I'm not thinking of leaving Chorley, Mrs. Hutton,' Tina said stiffly. 'I'm quite satisfied with the job I've got.'

'That so?' Again Sarah was running a speculative eye round the sitting-room. 'If your Aunt Maudie left Chorley, you'd leave with her, I daresay.'

Tina's mouth went dry. She was right about these two! They hadn't travelled down from Birmingham solely out of concern for Aunt Maud. They had their acquisitive eyes on her house! On the money it would bring if it was sold!

They left in a while to lunch at the Tudor Arms. Afterwards they would go to the hospital and return here later . . . to take a sentimental look over her girlhood home, Sarah added coyly.

The blatant insincerity of the Huttons was so plain to Tina that she wanted to say outright to Aunt Maud, the following afternoon at the hospital, that they were interested in only one thing in Chorley . . . the house Aunt Maud had been left by her father, now worth three times its original value. She fumed inwardly at the fuss Sarah made of Aunt Maud. She had bought her a fluffy pink bedjacket and insisted she put it on. Tina's hothouse grapes were left unnoticed on the bedside locker.

'There, pink's your colour, Maudie,' Sarah gushed, and Tina, unable to bear any more of this, swung on her heel and hurried out to the corridor.

'You can go in if you like,' she said, to Sidney Hutton, who was smoking a cigarette beside an open window.

'Oh, let's leave them to natter—I'd sooner stay and talk to you, little lady.' He smirked a smile down at her and displayed an ornate gold cigarette-case, at which Tina shook her head. As he slipped the case back into his pocket his glance travelled over Tina, who was wearing a neat brown coat that set off her fair hair. Her beige handbag matched her shoes.

'Thought any more about coming up north to live?' he asked, dropping his voice into a low, intimate key.

She looked at him, taking in his pomaded self-importance and the gold watch-chain stretched across his broad chest. 'I shouldn't think for a minute that Aunt Maud will want to leave Dulcey Avenue,' she replied stiffly. 'She's too used to Chorley and its quiet atmosphere.'

'The place must be a bit dull for a pretty

girl like you.' His thick mouth moved in a smile. 'Y'know, you could have a lot of fun working for me.' He lowered her a meaning wink. 'I'm a generous man to the—people I like.'

The brand of generosity to which he was referring sent a wave of nausea through Tina, and she moved sharply away from him. The thought of working for such a man, of probably living in the same house, was quite unbearable. Also she knew a fierce desire to protect her aunt from what he and his wife obviously had in mind; they were a pair of sharks, and at the earliest opportunity Aunt Maud must be talked out of trusting them.

She decided, however, not to broach this ticklish subject until Aunt Maud had undergone her operation, which went off smoothly a few days later and was unaccompanied by complications. On the Friday evening, with her aunt looking very much better, Tina quietly tackled her about the Huttons.

'Be careful of them, Aunt Maud,' she said, hands nervously clenched as she sat in the bedside chair. 'I believe they're only after the money you'll get for your house if you sell it.'

A silence hung between Maud Manson and her young niece, so very different in looks and disposition, then the corded, elderly hands drew the fluffy bedjacket closer around the rawboned shoulders. The dark eyes narrowed, hard as stones in the plain, bitter face. 'That's a very nice thing to say about my sister and brother-in-law.' Maud Manson's voice matched her eyes. 'I suppose you were hoping I'd die and *you'd* get my bit of money? Well, for all your eagerness to get me into this place, I'm still alive and kicking.'

The deliberate, acid cruelty of these remarks drove every scrap of colour out of Tina's cheeks. She sat stunned. If her aunt had suddenly given her two hard blows round the face she couldn't have felt more hurt.

'Don't look at me with crocodile tears in your eyes,' Maud Manson snapped. 'I made up my mind that day I came into this hospital that I was going to write to Sarah. If anything had happened to me, she's more entitled to what I've got than *you* are. You make out that butter wouldn't melt in your mouth, but as Sarah says, it's all put on. She was telling me last Sunday how you sulked just because she wanted to see over the house, for old times' sake.'

'She wanted to assess its value, not to relive old memories.' Tina was still shaking with pain as she pushed back her chair and got to her feet. 'Are you going to sell up and go to Birmingham, Aunt Maud?' she asked flatly.

'Any objections?' Maud Manson's eyes were sharp and malignant. 'Is it so wrong that I should want company after you've grabbed some fool man and gone off with him? I know that's all you're waiting for—like all the rest—like your chit of a mother!'

For years Tina had tolerated unkind remarks about the young mother she could not remember, but all of a sudden, on top of her aunt's growing bitterness towards herself, they were insupportable.

'You've never felt a spark of affection for me in all the years I've lived with you, have you, Aunt Maud?' she said shakily. 'I've always known, but out of gratitude to you for giving me a home I've tried not to mind. Well, I have minded. All children need and expect affection, but you denied it to me because you chose to object to your brother falling in love and marrying. Now, because I've grown to look like my mother, you have to keep jabbing at me. I don't have to put up with that—and I'm not going to. Nor do I intend to come to Birmingham to be the Huttons' underpaid drudge!'

'I don't know where else you think you're going.' Maud Manson grunted. 'But if that's how you feel, then suit yourself. I've done my best for you. Sacrificed the best years of my life bringing up another woman's child—'

'I'm grateful for the home you've given me, Aunt Maud,' Tina broke in, 'but I—I can't come to Birmingham. If you decided to stay here in Chorley it would be a different matter—'

'I'm going to Birmingham,' was the tart retort. 'Sidney knows someone who will give me a good price for my bit of property.'

Tina didn't doubt it for a moment, while she tiredly told herself that if Aunt Maud wanted the Huttons, then there was nothing more to be said. It was obvious she had made up her mind, while if Tina had not quite made up hers, as to where she was going, she had made it up with regard to her aunt's sister and brother-in-law. She didn't want to work for them, or live anywhere near them!

*   *   *

A cold scatter of rain met Tina as she turned out of the hospital gates. When she reached the market square she went into an espresso bar which had replaced an old established tea-room and ordered a cup of coffee. She sipped its sweet frothiness, her thoughts and emotions in a quiet turmoil. Had she the right, let alone the courage, to walk out on her aunt after all these years? Her gaze turned towards the window beside her and she saw across the square the board of the Tudor Arms swinging in the wind. A chiffon of rain veiled the black and white timbering and plaster of the inn—there on the cobbles fronting it she had said good-bye to John Trecarrel.

She recalled the things he had said to her. She knew that if he were here right now he would say she had done the right thing in standing up to her tyrannical aunt at long last. 'You're free to go your own way,' he would say. 'Haven't you the grit to grab the chance now it's within your grasp?'

Free! To leave Chorley . . . for London.

Excitement stirred within her. She knew in this moment that she would do it, she would go to the big city instead of just dreaming about it on Chorley's headland. In the strangest fashion, as she made this decision, she seemed to feel again the firm grip of John Trecarrel's fingers. His hands had been one of the nicest things about him—on the left hand, on the third finger, she hadn't missed the Gothic gold band which had told her he was married. His wife's name had been Joanna. Tina knew because she had looked up the information in *Who's Who* in the library. Joanna Lizabeth, daughter of the late Colonel Hillard Carrish of Brinsham, Devon.

Joanna Carrish had married John Trecarrel when she was twenty and he twenty-seven. Two years later she had given birth to a daughter, Lizabeth. A year later Joanna had died while yachting with friends off the coast of Ste. Monique.

The death of John Trecarrel's wife had occurred eight years ago, and because of those deep lines engraved beside his mouth, Tina guessed how much he had loved her—how much he missed her. She had been beautiful, of course, leaving him with the inability to love again as he had the living loveliness of Joanna. She had been gay and full of life and she had probably called him Johnny ... and out of his painful knowledge he had said to Tina:

'Youth is such a short and precious time. Don't waste it.'

* * *

Tina travelled to London a week later, armed with a glowing reference from her Chorley employers, and an address given to her by one of the girls with whom she had worked. The girl's cousin was employed in London and living in a Kensington hostel for business girls. Tina might be lucky enough to get a room there.

She took a bus to the hostel straight from the railway station, and half an hour later was unpacking her suitcase in a back box of a room only recently vacated. The hostel was a tall Georgian house not far from Kensington High Street, and Tessa Neal, who came from Chorley herself, turned out to be a pleasant, friendly girl.

The following evening she took Tina for a stroll round London and was naturally interested in what she was going to do about a job. Tessa worked in a typing agency, where she said there was always room for a speedy typist. But Tina, comfortably aware of the holiday cheque in her handbag, felt like treating herself to a week's exploration of the big city before she settled down again behind the keyboard of a typewriter.

'I'd rather like to have a look round before making up my mind, Tessa,' she hedged, for also, having gone through the agony of learning shorthand at evening classes, she felt she'd like to try for a secretarial post. Once she was experienced as a secretary she might be able to get a job in Canada or Australia. Her heartbeats quickened at such an exciting possibility.

'Anyway, I'll tell our superintendent about you,' Tessa smiled. 'I know my cousin liked working with you.'

To a newcomer, London has many attractions to offer, foremost to a girl its fabulous shops. Tina spent the following morning dazzling her eyes along Oxford Street and the Burlington Arcade. She lunched at a Bistingo and felt madly sophisticated sitting alone, in the heart of London, enjoying tomato soup, a grill, and a banana-split. Afterwards she jumped on a bus for Hyde Park, where she strolled along beside the Serpentine and had tea at a little outdoor café.

It was on her way back to the hostel that a sudden breathtaking idea occurred to her for the following day. She would go to the gallery where she knew John Trecarrel's West Indian bronzes were still on view. Seeing his work would be a little like seeing him again. It was a month since they had talked on the headland at Chorley and she guessed that by now he would have returned to his home on the island of Ste. Monique.

Blue Water House. An imaginative name, conjuring up a picture of graciousness and charm in Tina's mind. The house stood near the ocean and you could hear the silvery breakers rolling over a coral reef, hear them crash open, expelling their lovely smell of ozone. There were many flowers, flame creepers, starry frangipani, and bright scarves of bougainvillea . . .

Tina gave a sigh and dragged her wandering thoughts back to the hostel. She must wear something nice for her trip to the gallery—she opened the narrow built-in wardrobe and took stock of the two new suits Kitty had persuaded her to buy. They had been inexpensive but were quite attractive. One was in French navy with touches of white, the other was a crisp houndstooth mixture of topaz, brown, and smoke-blue. She had a smoke-blue silk-knit jersey to go with this suit—yes, she would wear the houndstooth!

When she was dressed, around eleven o'clock the following morning, she looked almost pretty with her hair held back in a mock-tortoiseshell slide and a dash of lipstick brightening her mouth. She chivvied her reflection when she saw how bright-eyed and expectant she looked. '*He* won't be there, my girl!' she said. 'Good lord, the man is far, far away, and *you* are a lost memory as far as he's concerned.'

She decided to make this a real treat and upon reaching the High Street she hailed a taxi. She gave the driver the name of the gallery, then sank back to enjoy the novelty of riding through London in style.

It was a bright April morning, with waves of sunshine breaking on the pavements where people strolled or hurried, and she saw a barrow in a side street laden with bunches of tulips and bachelor's buttons. The taxi turned into a road that seemed lined at either side with antique shops, they passed some delightful houses, then an embankment which Tina correctly guessed to be the Chelsea Embankment. A minute later she was fumbling with the door handle, nervously excited as she handed the driver his fare. The gallery was smart and modern-looking, with plate-glass, platter-knobbed doors, and Tina pushed through them on to carpet that was as softly green and yielding as a new-mown lawn.

She paid her entrance fee and walked forward into the long gallery. There were quite a few people looking at the bronzes, but their voices were muted, as in a museum or a library. The Trecarrel works of art were arranged on pedestal stands.

Tina wandered from one to the other, and it came to her that showy words like brilliant and exciting couldn't be applied to creations such as these. They had that same vitality that had struck her about the man responsible for them; a fresh-muscle-bone look that made her feel they would be warm to the touch. She was warmed, stirred, unsurprised by the artistry which had fashioned the dusky Negroid head at which she was looking, when a couple of men strolled down the staircase in the centre of the gallery.

One was plumpish and clad in a morning

coat over striped trousers; there was an air of satisfaction about him, for he rubbed his hands together as he talked and wore an unctuous smile. His tall companion fixed Tina's gaze—those tanned, irregular features and darkly lashed blue eyes were unmistakable. She was looking at John Trecarrel. Perhaps, unconsciously, she gave a small gasp, and he heard it, for in that moment he looked at her. A black eyebrow quirked above a sea-blue eye, then recognition dawned in his eyes. He said something to the man beside him, then three long strides had brought him to Tina.

'The girl on the cliff!' His fingers clicked. 'Tina Morton?'

'Manson.' Her laugh was tremulous, and as their hands met she noticed the faultless tailoring of his grey town suit and how distinguished he looked with his hair brushed smooth so that the small wings of silver glinted at his temples.

'Well, this is a surprise!' he exclaimed, smiling down at her. 'Have you taken a day off from work to come and see my exhibits?'

She shook her head. 'I-I've left Chorley—for good!' she blurted.

'What's that?' He bent lower as in

sudden acute shyness she glanced away from him, towards a long, silver-grey fish with tigerish teeth. The bared teeth looked ready to snap at her. Then John Trecarrel took hold of her chin and made her look at him. His eyes were every bit as blue as she remembered them ... his lean, dark, rather whimsical face was again doing the oddest things to her heart.

'You've snapped your leading string, eh?' he drawled. 'How interesting.'

She didn't quite understand the inflection in his voice, but his hand had dropped to her shoulder where it pressed her reassuringly into further speech. In a low, none too steady voice she told him what had led to her decision to come to London. 'I found it impossible to stay with my aunt any longer,' she wound up. 'I think she wanted me with her just to have the satisfaction of—of—'

'A whipping-girl,' John Trecarrel put in with that cruel-kind perceptiveness of his. 'Someone to take the lash for her, because in her narrow, bitter mind she blames everyone but herself for her loveless life. Good luck to you for getting out, Tina!' A smile ran those attractive creases beside his eyes. 'We must celebrate your emancipation—can you lunch with me?'

'I'd love to!' She flushed with pleasure at the suggestion.

'Good.' He gestured round the gallery. 'Seen all you want to see in here?'

'Well—would you take me round and tell me how you came to create each subject?' she asked eagerly.

'Child,' he broke into a slight laugh, while quite unexpectedly the colour deepened under his tanned skin, 'are you that interested?'

'Of course.' The smile that touched her mouth was gentle, more assured, for that faint flush of his made him very human . . . less of the deity who dwelt in regions far above those she could ever aspire to. 'I know hardly anything about sculpture, but yours have something breathing about them. Like that beautiful Rodin called "The Kiss."'

'H'm,' he grinned, 'no man worth his salt could resist that kind of flattery from a female. Come along then . . . now this fishy creature here is a barracuda, a sea tiger that hunts its prey in Caribbean waters . . .'

For almost an hour Tina toured the gallery with him. Some of the elegantly dressed visitors, socially prominent, from their speech and manner, made attempts to draw him into their smart cliques, but with a cool air of politeness he kept aloof, a hand at Tina's elbow. They were near the plate-glass doors when a woman in a rather fantastic hat called his name in a cooing but demanding voice.

'Come on!' he hissed at Tina, and the next moment the doors were swinging shut behind them and they were out on the pavement.

A few minutes later they were sitting in a sleek saxe-blue car and heading in the direction of the West End. They would lunch at a place called L'Aperitif, he decided, shooting a look over Tina's suit and neatly disposed legs when the car throbbed at some traffic signals.

She felt his glance. Her fingers curled over her clutch bag, her heart gave a curious throb as he moved the handbrake and brushed her with his arm.

'I quite thought that by now you'd be back on your island, Mr. Trecarrel,' she said, as the powerful car surged forward again.

'Friends and business contacts have kept me here rather longer than I planned.' A pause, with a hint of deliberation about it.

'A bit of luck, eh? We might not have met again.'

Despite the emotion that gripped her throat she was able to murmur a fairly steady reply, but as the sunshine glittered on the Gothic band on his left hand she found herself averting her eyes . . . as though from a warning signal she didn't want to take notice of.

CHAPTER TWO

'IT'S been quite a while since I came to England,' he said. 'I'm going home in ten days' time. I've promised Liza, she's my young daughter, to be home in time for the end of term holiday she gets from her school. She attends a boarding school and we don't see a lot of each other.'

He spoke fondly, but a glance at him showed Tina a dent between his eyebrows that could have meant that he worried about the child. 'Isn't her school on the island?' Tina asked.

'No, it's at Barbados. A bit of a way to send her, but there she mixes with British children. I wanted that for her rather than a cosmopolitan atmosphere, which I think creates too much precosity in a child. Or does that sound pompous?'

'It sounds sensible, and very loyal of you,' Tina smiled.

He turned into a narrow side road and spotting a space between a row of parked cars he braked there, but before opening the door to get out, he looked directly at Tina. 'I suppose, having taken this plunge into a brand new life, you're feeling nervous and out of your depth. Are you fixed up with a job yet?'

She shook her head. He was close enough for her to breathe his after-shave lotion, lemony and clean. The dent in his chin held a fingertip of shadow. His wide, rather beautiful mouth, lined at the sides, shook her heart as she looked at it. She suspected in this moment what was happening to her and could hardly bear to remember that after next week he would be gone from England's shores.

'Let's go and have lunch.' He threw open the car door. 'We should get a table.' And as they entered the restaurant, he caught the eye of the head waiter, who came over at once, greeting him by name and assuring them that a table would be available in half an hour. They went into a lounge where deep, low, velvet chairs were arranged beside informal tables with gay drink-coasters and amber-glass ashtrays on their glistening surfaces. Tina's heels sank into the carpeting as they walked to a pair of chairs in a secluded corner. They sat down and John Trecarrel beckoned a white-jacketed waiter.

'What do you fancy to drink?' he asked Tina.

She could only think of tomato juice or orange squash, and she nodded when he suggested a gin and ginger ale with ice. 'Sounds lovely,' she agreed.

'Daring, eh?' He was laughing at her, and she liked it. Liked him, this place, the whole marvellous world in this moment.

He ordered a Tom Collins for himself and when their drinks arrived, he settled back with a comfortable sigh. 'Now we can talk, uninterrupted by your flattering preoccupation with my busts and beasts, and those peculiar people who collect celebrities as more normal folk collect debts.' He raised his glass to Tina. 'Here's luck to you in London.'

'Thank you!' Then, half shyly, she added: 'Here's luck to you—on Ste.

Monique.'

He narrowed his eyes over the rim of his glass, his smile when it came on was a trifle bleak. Tina at once dropped her glance to the glass in her hand, watching the pieces of ice with their starburst centres.

'Drink up,' he said. 'Gin settles the nerves.'

So he knew she was on edge, even though she was enjoying being here with him? She took a cautious sip at her drink, found it quite enjoyable and took a deeper gulp.

'You mustn't go on feeling guilty because you've walked out on an intolerable situation, Tina,' he went on. 'After all, your aunt chose of her own free will to go north with these relatives of hers, so you haven't let her down in any way. I can't see you letting anyone down—you're rather the self-sacrificing sort, aren't you, child?'

She was startled into looking at him. He wasn't smiling. His face wore a sudden formidable look, his eyes gazing beyond her, back down the years, as though he were thinking of someone else with a similar disposition.

Tina wanted to touch his hand and say personal, impossible things, like: 'Don't let your memories hurt you, please. I know they can't be recaptured, but you have loved and been loved.'

As he came back out of his trance he raised a hand at the waiter, serving at a nearby table. 'Repeat, please!' His voice was harsh, his eyes narrow slits of fierce blue. Tina shivered and realized how little she knew of life and men. She felt, beside this man who had once loved deeply and passionately, like a gauche child.

'What kind of a job are you thinking of getting?' he asked.

'Oh—secretarial work.' This was a safe topic and she clutched eagerly at it. 'I am a shorthand-typist and I thought, if I acquire some experience as a secretary, I might try for a job abroad. I mean,' she gave a laugh and cradled the cold, slender glass that held her drink, 'I might as well see something of the world now—now I'm free.'

'I know one or two businessmen in London, maybe I could help you get a job . . . ah, thanks!' he turned to pay the waiter for his drink, and when he glanced back at Tina, he broke into a sardonic smile at the wide-eyed way she was regarding him. 'It's all right, I have no ulterior motive,' he drawled meaningly.

'Oh, I know!' She flushed and her confused gaze ran down the tiny silver anchors spattering his tie. 'I didn't mean—'

'Blast my tongue!' He put a quick hand across the table and, after a momentary hesitation, Tina slipped her cold one into its waiting warmth. His lean fingers closed tight and hard about hers. 'Men can be damnable brutes—it's been, you see, a long time since I've known someone like you. Forgive me?'

She nodded, but she was thinking of Sidney Hutton and what he would have expected in exchange for his offer of employment. Was it inevitable that the bitterness you learned from others must sour fresh associations, budding friendships? Couldn't you trust to instinct? It seemed you couldn't. She *had* wondered for a wild moment why John Trecarrel, a famous celebrity of the art world, should show an interest in a country mouse of a typist.

'What are you thinking?' he demanded.

'You're being very kind to me, Mr. Trecarrel. Giving me lunch, offering to find me a job—'

'You're lost and lonely, like a big-eyed kitten.' He broke into a grin. 'Wouldn't I do the same for a kitten?'

She had to laugh, and after that was more relaxed with him. They dined at a wallside table, below a long mirror, where they shared a comfortable cushioned seat. Their waiter presented them with large menu cards, with L'Aperitif lettered in dashing gold across the front of them.

Tina felt her companion's glance, then he came suddenly closer to her and helped her select her meal. He was all charm, now, consulting with the wine waiter on a suitable white wine to accompany their salmon cutlets. It was delicious, sending a glow through Tina's veins, and before she could stop him the waiter had refilled her glass as their chaudfroid of chicken arrived at the table, accompanied by heart of lettuce and ruby rings of tomato. They finished the meal with sliced peaches in kirsch, then dark coffee in doll-sized cups.

'Do you miss the sea now you're in London?' John Trecarrel asked, facing Tina with a lazy smile, the tension gone out of him.

'I expect I shall later on,' she admitted. 'Right now I'm fascinated by the shops and the crowds.'

'But fundamentally you aren't a crowd

person, eh? Where are you staying, at a girls' hostel?'

She nodded.

'You didn't leave any boy-friends back in Chorley, I take it?'

'Oh, no.' Her grin was impish. 'I'm not exactly the sort boys go for. I mean, they like glamour, don't they?'

'Do they?' His smile grew quizzical. 'It's a long time since I was a boy. I'm thirty-nine, Tina. Does that seem a great age to you?'

'Of course not.' She looked surprised, for he didn't seem the sort of man who worried much about his personal effect on people, least of all on someone as unsophisticated as herself. Were she a soignée woman of the world . . . then he might be curious about the impression he was making on her.

'What sort of a man do you think I am, Tina?' His eyes held hers, a definite curiosity in them. 'Kind, thoughtful, generous?'

'Yes,' she said, and she couldn't add that she also thought him an unhappy one.

'Yes,' he agreed, 'I'm all three. Most men are—with certain reservations. They can also be unthinking, possessive and cruel.'

'Are you warning me to be careful of the men I—I might meet up here in London?' Tina queried, flushing slightly in case he was also warning her not to develop a youthful crush on *him*, merely because he showed her a little passing concern and kindness.

His left eyebrow quirked above an aqua-blue eye. 'Forgive the lecture,' he drawled. 'The life you led down in Chorley has kept you young for your years in some respects, and though boys of your own age might be dazzled by surface glitter, there are older men who prefer shyness and a lack of sophistication. And mature men, my child, often know how to charm the shyest bird off her perch. They know they represent the father-figure, one of the most subtle and potent dangers young, lonely things like you can encounter.'

'Well, thanks for the lecture,' she half laughed, 'but I'm not a child. I know the difference between genuine kindness in a man and the other thing.'

'No, you don't.' A look of tired exasperation crossed his face. 'You haven't a clue why I've given you lunch, and why I'm going to ask you to spend the afternoon with me.'

Her eyes widened. The startled leap of her heart parted her lips as her breath caught.

He pulled a mocking face at her. 'I want to buy some presents for Liza, and you'll know better than I what will appeal to a young female thing of nine years. I don't imagine she still wants dolls and tea-sets, do you?'

Tina shook her head. A smile was spreading over her face. *He* might be unthinking, possessive and cruel, but not today, not to her! Nothing else mattered beyond this moment, that he not only asked her to spend the afternoon with him, but he wanted to share with her the intimacy of buying presents for his child.

'Is Lizabeth like you?' she asked, when they were driving towards Piccadilly.

'Yes, she's a Trecarrel,' he replied. 'She was rather an enchanting moppet when she was small, now, of course, she's at the leggy, intense stage. A man knows what to do with babies, he just dandles them, but as they grow older they develop fads that are a little harder to understand and handle. Girls, the eternal mystery to man.' He shot a grin at Tina, who met it, as neatly curled beside him as a small cat. She had her own mystique, as most girls have with her smoky eyes and the fragile tilt to her cheekbones. Her porcelain-pink lip colouring emphasized the heart shape of her mouth.

'I have a Corot back home on the island, of a flaxen-haired child reading by a lamp,' John Trecarrel said. 'You could have sat for it. The facial bones have a similar shadowed delicacy—ah, I want to stop here at Dunhill's for some tobacco!'

He left her in the car while he went into the shop, and, not normally curious about her looks, Tina sat up and stared at her reflection in the mirror of the little tidy-table in front of her. By no stretch of the imagination could she be called pretty, and with a rueful laugh she sank back in her seat and gazed out of the window beside her. She could see John Trecarrel through the big window of Dunhill's. He was talking to the man behind the counter, at ease, tall and distinguished in his impeccable grey suit. A man from another world, who said charming, casual things, like that about the Corot, without meaning them to be taken seriously. It was a subtle man-woman language and he must momentarily have forgotten that Tina was as much a stranger to it as she was to Hebrew.

She watched him stride out of the shop, and as he came to the car, Tina felt her nails digging into her clutch bag. So this was what made Kitty Longway's cheeks turbulently pink, and Tessa Neal's eyes wistfully glow—a man—that mysterious force that clicked a little switch inside a woman and made her light up.

He slid in beside her and gave her that quick smile that crinkled his eyes. He didn't speak, and there was for Tina an unnerving enchantment to the moment. For now, for this brief span of time, he was content to be with her, and his smile told her so.

They drove to Dickins and Jones, where he consulted his daughter's measurements in a notebook and gave Tina free choice in a selection of smart outfits for the child. She was particularly taken with some pierrot pyjamas and he laughingly agreed that Liza would appreciate the fun of them. Then at Swaine and Adeney he bought her a saddle. Liza was a good little horsewoman, he said, and something clutched hard at Tina's throat. She saw the child, leggy and intense, stretching up to be a womanly companion for her lonely father when she was home from school. She saw him, riding a hunter beside his daughter's pony, his glance upon the young head and certain things about her—though she was a Trecarrel—bringing her mother vividly alive for him.

At Boucheron's in Bond Street he bought a slim jewelled bracelet, delicate as a chain of dewdrops, and asked for it to be inscribed with three simple words. My dear daughter.

As the assistant made a note of the inscription, John Trecarrel stepped to an adjacent counter where there was a display of jewelled compacts, chunky costume rings, personality charms, etc. He picked up a butterfly brooch, a pretty blue thing, the wings a pair of aquamarines joined by a silver body. 'I'll take this as well,' he said to the assistant, and casually and easily he pinned the brooch to the collar of Tina's suit.

'Mr. Trecarrel,' she gasped, 'I can't—'

'Miss Manson,' he mockingly imitated her wide-eyed alarm, 'you must.'

'M-must I?'

He nodded, amused and obviously quite

determined.

They had tea at Harrods, where his eyes teased her unmercifully. Then all too soon they were driving along Kensington High Street, straight into the rose and gold of the sunset. His dark face was gilded to a medieval quality, and she saw below her left eye the blink of the brooch he had given her. In a few more minutes he would be saying good-bye to her, and as daylight trailed out of the sky so did joy trail out of Tina. Good-bye—blue and melancholy as the twilight creeping over London's rooftops.

The car drew in before the hostel and he turned to look at her. 'Do you think you'd enjoy an exhibition of watercolours and woodcuts?' he inquired casually.

The jewelled sunset colours had faded. Out of the shadows his eyes alone were discernible, blue as the aquamarine wings over which her fingers closed.

'Well, Tina?'

'Yes,' she said, her heart pounding.

'Then I'll call for you at noon tomorrow. We'll lunch together, go to the exhibition—or anywhere else you fancy.'

'No, the exhibition sounds lovely, Mr. Trecarrel. Thank you for asking me.'

'What a polite, quaint young thing you are.' He put a hand over hers, and it was lost, gone under, as she was. Powerless to fight the fascination he had for her. 'Thank you for this afternoon. You have a natural quality of detachment, Tina, which allows a man his thoughts.'

He swung out of the car and came round to open the door beside her. She stepped out, his hand on her arm, slipping down until his fingers found hers. 'I'll see you tomorrow, child.'

She gave a low, happy laugh and he echoed it. That very male sound was warming and delightful—she could never have believed that anything could give her so much pleasure. She ran up the steps of the hostel, looking back as the sleek saxe-blue car slid away into the twilight, gemmed with London lights.

* * *

A lyrical interval had begun for Tina, and as each day came, she didn't look beyond it. There was the exhibition and afterwards Holland Park Gardens where peacocks flaunted their jewelled tails, and the lake mirrored the golden grace of the willows.

One evening the haunting throb of gipsy violins and the flickering candlelight of a Hungarian restaurant tucked away in Chelsea.

He discovered she liked music and took her to a concert. The final moments of a Beethoven symphony left her enclosed in a core of silent wonder, and so she sat, the chords of the music echoing in her mind, while the car sped out of London on to the straight stretch of the Hog's Back. The countryside rolled away at either side of them, mysteriously tinged with the glow of a crescent moon, looking not unlike a small boat poised in the act of descending a dark river. Tina turned dreaming eyes to John's profile, a hard, dark silhouette against that milky glow shed by the moon. John, at once charming and aloof, responsive to gaiety, but haunted by a lovely ghost.

She had been lovely. Quite casually, in fact, had it slipped out. Attending an art auction at Christie's with him, Tina had commented on the beauty of an eighteenth-century model who had sat for a series of miniatures. 'Faultless profiles are quite common,' he had replied 'The test is to see the owners full face. Joanna—my wife, you know—was beautiful at every angle.'

He had gone on to talk about something else, but Tina could not forget his words. They had been spoken without sentimentality, for only in stories and films did people violate the secrecy of their love by saying things like: 'She was the most beautiful creature I ever saw, and when she died much of my heart died with her.'

The car sighed to a standstill at this point in her reflections and she saw that he had parked on a grass verge near a small stone bridge. Now the engine was quiet the peacefulness was complete. The babbling of water under the bridge did not intrude on it, while the night air was drenched with the scent of the wild roses that clung in sleeping clusters to the hedges.

John faced her, stretching an arm along the seat. She felt the tips of his fingers against her shoulder, and light though his touch was, it sent tiny currents thrilling through her. She had an impulse to lean back and feel his arm about her, enclosing her in an arc of warmth and protection. They sat like that for several minutes, content to listen to the country sounds, then all at once John's fingers were gripping her shoulder.

'Tina,' he spoke rather tensely, 'do you

like me?'

Her breath caught in her throat. Her hands found each other in her lap and clung together. The world was whirling and she could feel it. 'Yes—I like you,' she replied huskily.'

Like? This captivation she felt whenever a smile lit his eyes and lines crinkled beside their vivid blue. This fire that ran through her veins at his nearness. She didn't just like him—she loved him!

And then he said: 'Do you like me enough to marry me?'

The words hung in the air, like the big bat that flitted by the car lights, an etching that pulsated for moments on end, then winged out of sight.

'Tina,' his voice and his grip had roughened, 'say something, even if it's only to tell me to go to the devil. What is it, has my proposal shocked you? Do you feel it's presumptuous of me because I'm so much older than you?'

She stared at him. In the moonglow his face was angular, the well-defined bones jutting hard under his skin, and everything in her cried out against separation from him. He had become so very dear to her, with his face that could look so moody, his smile that could warm the moodiness away, his voice with its deep tones. But she didn't think he loved her.

'We're strangers,' she heard herself say at last. 'Strangers don't marry.'

There was a long silence and she could hear something ticking—his watch! 'Some people, Tina,' he spoke almost harshly, 'are never strangers because from the first words they speak they're friends. I thought you understood that. I thought your intelligence a cut above that of some of today's self-obsessed youngsters.'

'Friends don't marry, either,' she said faintly.

'You're too young to know that there can be a hundred reasons why people get married.' His voice, now, was faintly weary, as though she disappointed him. 'Marriage with me, in this instance, is surely a better proposition than a humdrum office job, and I can throw in a couple of bonuses—Ste. Monique and a home of your own.'

'Don't!' The appeal broke from her. 'I thought you kind, but you're like everyone else, you think my shyness gives you a licence to enjoy a spot of bullying. Y-you wouldn't do it with someone older, lovelier, smarter—'

'If you were those three things, my child, I shouldn't be proposing to you.' He pulled her to him until her cold young face was pressing his. 'I've grown boorish in my loneliness, you see. I need a wife.'

It was his use of the word loneliness that weakened her resistance, his nearness that breached it. Never in her wildest dreams had she envisaged a moment such as this, when John Trecarrel would hold her and talk of marriage. She felt his hand on her hair ... no one had ever stroked her hair ... no one had ever really wanted her until this moment ...

'I thought you liked me,' he murmured. 'I like you, Tina. Isn't it enough?'

It was heaven, when she had only ever hoped for a few more days with him. Now, if she chose, she could be with him on his island ... never again be lonely herself.

'Are you dozing down there?' he queried.

She gave a sobbing little laugh at the note of humour in his voice. 'You can't be serious, John,' she said. 'I have no beauty, no wit, no experience to give to a man like you.'

'You only have amenity, sensitivity, and

a lack of selfishness, my dear.' His fingertips travelled over the delicate bones of her face, his warm, clever, speaking hands slid round till they spread themselves against the thin thrust of her shoulderblades. He brought her closer to him and her lips waited, soft and innocently untried. She trembled, as though struck through by pain or lightning, as she felt the first kiss of her life. She was held in suspense, it drifted like a feather, then all of her was crying and seared and awake. She clung to the only solidity in her whirling world, his shoulders. All else was sensation. She hadn't known what she was capable of feeling. She drowned in her awakening which was also a kind of death—the death of immaturity and girlhood.

Gone was all logical thinking. She was caught too strongly now by the magic of this moment to care what might lie beyond it.

'So the answer's yes?' She heard the smile in his voice, her cheek was locked against his and she couldn't see his eyes.

'If you want me, John,' she whispered.

Please, have no regrets, she prayed. Be glad, not sorry, that you asked me to marry you and I accepted.

He held her away from him. 'We'll be married next week,' he spoke matter-of-factly. 'I'll apply for a special licence.'

'Will Liza mind, do you think?' she asked shyly.

'A little, perhaps, at the beginning. But once she gets to know you—' he brushed at a strand of her flaxen hair. 'You must have a trousseau, Tina, but don't go messing about with you hair. Leave it as it is. It's part of your charm, what I noticed first that afternoon on the cliff, blowing in the wind, the only part of you that was free. Poor Tina, little girl lost. Are you still lost, I wonder?'

He put a kiss against her left eyebrow, then turned to start the car. On the way back to London he talked about Blue Water House, bringing its loveliness alive for her. She saw the bougainvillea that clouded mellowed walls with vivid, entrancing colour. The blossoms that slumbered in the sun like richly clad beauties, the feathery palms that dusted the aquamarine sky, the giant bushes of luscious hibiscus, poking scarlet tongues from big peach bells. Their rich, heavy scents were in her notrils.

Blue Water House was of the Colonial era, John said, when there had been rich sugar plantations on the island, worked by dusky African slaves. The house was so named because it stood on a hill that commanded a wide view of the blue sea.

'You mustn't feel nervous about being its châtelaine.' John gave her a quick look. 'I employ an efficient staff of servants, and though they'll expect to take their orders from the new "missus", you'll find them pleasant enough to deal with. I've a feeling they'll like the idea of Mr. John having a young, pretty wife.'

Tina knew she wasn't pretty, but it was nice that John should say so. 'To love is a greater thing than to be loved.' She must have read that in a book at some time and she could only hope that it was true. I love him, she thought. I'm going to marry him. I'm going to be the second Mrs. Trecarrel. She watched his profile and her love for him was a joy and a pain in her—for he had said: 'I like you, Tina. Isn't it enough?'

The car drew into the kerb in front of the hostel and, taking her cold hands into his, he gave them a rub to warm them and told her that he had a friend in London, a Mrs. Gaye Lanning, who would be happy to help her shop for her trousseau. Then there were her engagement and weddding rings to buy.

He felt the half apprehensive, half excited tremor that shook her and, laughing low in his throat, he drew her into his arms. 'You aren't afraid of me, are you?' he mocked.

Yes, she wanted to admit. His was a subtle, complex, brooding personality. She never really knew what he was thinking or planning. She guessed, too, that he had a temper, an icy one that could lock her out in the cold.

'Marriage, Tina, is a sublime madness and a gamble for a man as well as a woman,' he said. 'Hasn't it occurred to you that in my own way I'm a trifle nervous of you?'

'Of *me*?' she echoed incredulously.

'You're many years younger than I, Tina. But, dammit, a man gets lonely, and you don't chatter and intrude—' His hands tightened on her. 'You're certain you want to marry me?'

She was certain of nothing—she only knew that from the moment on the headland at Chorley, when she had turned and looked into his eyes, she had started on a journey that would lead her to heaven or agony.

'Yes, I want to marry you, John,' she replied quietly.

He kissed her, and she no longer cared what might be lying in wait for her over the horizon, in the house that had been Joanna's.

* * *

Mrs. Lanning turned out to be a pleasant person in her late thirties. Her husband, a publicity executive, had been at Oxford with John and they had been friends ever since. Tina guessed that Gaye must have known Joanna, but if it surprised her that John had chosen to marry someone so different from his lovely first wife, she concealed the fact and was kindness itself to Tina during the next few days.

Aware that as Mrs. John Trecarrel she would have a position to uphold, Tina didn't argue when he told Gaye to take her to a really good couture house for her trousseau. 'Have fun and don't count the cost, Gaye,' he laughed.

'Bliss!' Gaye laughed back 'A lovely shopping spree without Chuck yelling at me to watch the bills. Why is it you men indulge your brides and deny your wives?'

'Something to do with the gilt shaking off the gingerbread,' Chuck Lanning put in from behind a wide-spread newspaper.

'That, Tina, is what you'll have to put up with after a few years,' Gaye warned. 'the fussing and cooing doesn't last.'

John quirked a dark eyebrow at Tina. 'Well, do you want to run out on me now these two have shown you the darker side of the picture?' he inquired amusedly.

She smilingly shook her head, for Gaye and Chuck Lanning bore all the signs of a tried and comfortable happiness. At the dining-table he had casually complimented his wife on the apple-marshmallow pie she had made for dessert, and Tina had seen the quick leap of pleasure in Gaye's grey eyes. Only a wife who cared still baked pies for a husband who had provided her with a cook and a maid.

The following day, looking very smart in a caballero hat and a sleek black suit, Gaye took Tina to a fashion house in Knightsbridge. The place had a rather drab frontage, but once they stepped inside, a sea of silvery carpet stretched ahead of them, with coral velour seats glowing here and there. A girl at the reception desk rang for the Directrice, who had received a phone call from Gaye and was expecting them. She appeared, thin, elegant, greeting Gaye as a known customer. They mounted a flight of stairs to a showroom and there the Directrice appraised Tina from top to toe.

She must have guessed directly that never in her life before had Tina been in a place like this, and it was obvious she correctly assessed the price of Tina's Chorley bought suit, but her manner didn't change a fraction. She wasn't effusive, nor too business-like, but she exuded the fact that first and foremost she was interested in selling beautiful clothes, whether to a duchess or a typist, and Tina suddenly found herself relaxing and enjoying the novelty of all this.

'Please to be seated, Miss Manson.' Elegant fingers waved at a chair. 'We will show you a selection of our younger models.'

The colours of the polished cottons, the afternoon silks, were wonderful and outlandish. Tina could never have envisaged herself in pale orange silk with a design of creamy yucca blossoms on it, but neither Gaye nor the Directrice were in any doubt that the dress would suit her. Then there was another they said she *must* have, two deep crisp layers of snowy lace banded by a sash of topaz-pink, so simple to look at—until Tina tried it on.

The eyes of the Directrice lit up behind her jewelled spectacles. 'Perfection!' she smiled, her thumb and forefinger in a circle, her fingers upraised. 'The gown was made for you, mademoiselle.'

Tina gazed wide-eyed at herself in the long, three-angled mirror. The lace dress left her shoulders bare; below the skirt, which ended just under her knees, her legs were very slender and her ankles had a breakable look in high-heeled topaz-pink sandals.

'John is going to like that,' Gaye said mischievously. 'It has what is known as man appeal.'

Tina's smile was shy, quick, abstracted. She hardly recognized herself and wondered what Aunt Maud would have said, confronted by this brand new Tina. For a moment a sensation of panic overwhelmed her. She was plunging head first into a marriage that held dangerous undercurrents, and there was no one she could confide in. Gaye seemed not to have the slightest suspicion that John was marrying merely to escape loneliness; the fact that he was spending money so lavishly on Tina obviously indicated to her uncomplicated mind that he was indulgently in love with his prospective bride.

Gaye was thoroughly enjoying herself, well in tune with the exaggerated language of fashion and determined to take John at his word over the matter of not counting the cost of a sumptuous, whispering thing in honey-gold faille; an afternoon dress with a big Quaker-girl collar in chalk-white piqué; play outfits for the beaches at Ste. Monique; lingerie in water-lily tones; and a honeymoon negligée with a lace-over-silk bodice.

The suit that she and the Directrice chose between them for Tina to be married in was a smoky blue colour, with pie-crust trimming on the neat collar and cuffs. Like most garments that fit perfectly and seem subdued, it gave Tina an innocent allure that made her heart skip a beat. Her bag and shoes were a smoky grey, her hat a fragile white silk rose meshed in tulle.

'You'll need a hairdo,' Gaye said. 'No, I'm not suggesting anything drastic, just a soft upsweep for your rose to nestle on. How does that sound—will your lord and master approve?'

Swift colour ran up Tina's slender neck to the roots of her hair She had no defence against such references to John, and Gaye gently laughed at her and gave her an understanding hug. Downstairs in the boutique Gaye chose a couple of youthful perfumes, a selection of cosmetics, and various other knick-knacks, then they drove in a taxi to the Copper Grill and ate delicious steaks in a quiet, oak-panelled dining-room hung with antique copper and porcelain ornaments.

It was over coffee that Gaye said: 'You love John a great deal, don't you, Tina?'

Tina, shy in her love, uncertain of how much real happiness she could give him, lowered her eyes and nodded wordlessly.

'He's lucky to have found you,' Gaye remarked with sincerity.

'I'm not used to his kind of life,' Tina faltered. 'I—I worry dreadfully in case I make blunders and give people room to—oh, you know what I mean! His first wife was so lovely—I know she was. How can I hope to compete?'

'Don't try, my dear.' Gaye reached over

and patted her hand. 'Just be yourself and everyone will love you. Sophistication isn't a thing to strive after, and you obviously have what John wants in a wife. Chuck and I are thrilled that he's marrying again. He's a nice person, and Liza needs a mother.'

'I hope the child won't resent me in any way—' Then Tina gave a half ashamed laugh. 'There I go again, finding something else to worry about.'

'It's true children sometimes resent a stepmother,' Gaye agreed, 'but Liza was only a toddler when Joanna died, so she isn't in a position to make the comparisons you obviously feel John and other people are going to make. You're different from Joanna. Quite frankly she was incredibly lovely to look at, but if John had wanted a reflection of her—well, there's her cousin, Paula Carrish, who lives on the island. It's never been a secret that for years she has cared for him. She—'

There Gaye broke off and frowned thoughtfully at Tina. 'Do you know the details of Joanna's death? Has John talked about it to you?'

Tina, her heart thudding in her breast, shook her head.

'You should be told.' Gaye poured

herself another cup of coffee and fed sugar into it. 'She fell over the side of a friend's yacht and drowned. She could swim like a seal, but she cracked her head on a reef of underwater coral. Paula was with her, right beside her when the accident occurred. She was hysterical for hours afterwards. John saw the accident from a beach near Blue Water House and he swam out to try and save Joanna. He tore open the side of his leg on the coral and was attacked by a barracuda—all in all it was a very tragic business, with John nearly losing his own life and a lot of rumours to scar his mind as well—'

'Rumours?' Tina whispered.

'Yes, about him and Paula. There was nothing in it, of course, but you know what people are. She used to model for him, you see, but the rumours were ridiculous in view of how he felt about Joanna. Anyway,' Gaye broke into a quick smile, 'that's all over with. He's about to start a new life with you, and I'm sure it's going to be a happy one.'

Tina forced her mouth into a smile, but her heart was heavy. Ste. Monique was haunted not only by a lovely ghost, but a woman named Paula lived there who for years, Gaye said, had cared for John. She had been with Joanna when she died. Already for Tina, who was to be the second Mrs. Trecarrel, she was a faceless enemy.

Outside the restaurant Gaye spotted a flower barrow massy with deep violet lilac, and exclaimed that she must have a bunch. 'I can't resist it!' she told Tina. 'May is the month for it, of course.'

May! The proverbially unlucky month for entering into matrimony. Tina stood on that London pavement, the scent of the lilac drowning her as Gaye piled her arms with it. In fear, in supplication almost, Tina buried her face in the lilac. Gaye was gazing at her when she raised her head. 'Look, why don't you spend the next few days at our flat?' she suggested. 'We have a guest room and it will be nicer for you than being among strangers at that hostel. I mean, a girl is always a bit nervy before her wedding. Do you like the idea?'

'I love it!' Tears of quick gratitude sprang to Tina's eyes, which Gaye tactfully ignored as she flagged a taxi.

Tina collected her belongings from the hostel that evening, for she wanted to say good-bye to Tessa Neal. Tessa was thrilled by her forthcoming marriage, but she took it for granted Tina had known her fiancé much longer than a week. Tina didn't enlighten her. She knew it would strike other people as little short of madness that in the course of a week she had fallen in love and pledged her future to a comparative stranger.

It was fantastic, she admitted to herself. A sort of landslide that was carrying her willy-nilly with it. She couldn't fight or scramble clear of the exciting, gathering momentum . . .

The following day she went with John to an exclusive Bond Street jewellers, where at a table covered in dark velvet, satin-lined trays of rings were laid out so that she might select her engagement ring. They were all equally lovely and dazzling, and Tina hardly dared select one in case it was an exorbitant price. She sat there in a straight-backed chair, John standing beside her, bending with a quizzical smile over the rings.

'Come on, darling,' he urged, 'what do you fancy? That sapphire solitaire is rather stunning, or how about this emerald-cut diamond?'

But her fingers, as though they couldn't help themselves, were hovering above a half-moon hoop of small, glowing, deep-red stones. The ring hadn't the dazzle of the others, therefore she felt sure this couldn't be as expensive. 'This is rather nice,' she murmured.

'Then let's try it on you.' John took it out of its satin bed and slipped it on to her finger. It fitted perfectly and the glow of the stones was intensified against the whiteness of her hand. 'It is pretty,' John gripped her hand and smiled down into her eyes. 'Do you want it?'

'Please!' She nodded eagerly.

The manager of the shop let out a small satisfied sigh. 'The young lady has exquisite taste, sir,' he remarked. 'I think one might say that rubies are the lovliest of the more precious gems.'

Rubies! Tina glanced up at John in a quiet panic, but his smile was still easy and indulgent. 'Now we'll see some wedding rings,' he said. 'Gold, eh, Tina?'

She nodded. It was just beginning to occur to her that John must have quite a bit of money, and she hoped that he didn't think she had chosen her ring because it was expensive. Oh dear, the simplest things seemed to have the costliest price tags, like some of those dresses at the fashion house yesterday. Her wedding suit, for instance, had cost far more than the gold faille or the white lace.

An assistant brought a tray of wedding rings to the table and it was John who selected her ring, a fairly wide band delicately engraved with a blossom design. She tried it on, her heart suddenly melting and warm inside her. John must care a little for her. His fingers, as she held out her hand to survey its gold and ruby burdens, were gripping her shoulder. She glanced up at him, and happiness ran out of her heart. His smile had gone and there was a strange tinge of whiteness about his mouth.

He was remembering that other wedding ring, the one he had bought for Joanna, the one that had glittered on her hand as she sank below the coral reef beyond Blue Water House . . .

Tina slipped the rings off her finger and laid them on the dark velvet.

'Put your engagement ring back on,' John said sharply.

But she stared at it. No, she wanted to say, no, you don't love me. I can't wear it—I can't marry you.

'Put it on,' he said again. His blue eyes challenged hers. He seemed to know what was screaming through her heart and her mind. 'Come, let me put it on.' His voice, his touch, were abruptly gentle and the ring was back on her hand—like a shackle, she thought wildly.

She watched him as he wrote out a cheque, then, followed by the effusive good wishes of the manager, they walked out to the street. Silently, side by side, they made for the meter where he had parked the car. This isn't how it should be, she told herself tearfully. We should be walking arm in arm, his fingers over mine, skimming little side smiles at each other . . .

'I'm glad you're staying with Gaye until the wedding,' he remarked. 'It was good of her to suggest it.'

'Yes,' Tina agreed. 'She's very nice.'

'Everything has happened almost too quickly for you, hasn't it, Tina?'

She knew his glance was upon her, but she kept on looking straight ahead. If I look a him, she thought, I'll disintegrate into a mere throb of love, there'll be nothing of me left, and it isn't fair that this should happen to me when nothing like it happens to him. Why does he want me? Because I don't chatter, because I don't intrude? No, I'll never intrude on his love for Joanna. He can take me or leave me, and that's why he wants me!

'I hope you aren't getting cold feet,' he drawled, touching her elbow with light fingers as they crossed a road. 'The announcement's in *The Times*. I've cabled Liza, and fixed our wedding date for Friday. All right?'

She nodded. They passed a record shop, and *Stranger on the Shore* wailed out. The melody caught her heart in a fist. She would marry John, but she knew that her love would never be strong enough to keep him from wandering 'the silent shore of memory'.

CHAPTER THREE

TINA discovered in the next few days that you didn't just board a plane and fly to the Caribbean. There was her passport to see to, and she was also compelled to have a vaccination against smallpox—a slightly unnerving business, offset by a visit to Gaye's hairdresser, where her hair was shampooed and styled into a soft, silvery upsweep. Tina gazed at herself in the mirror, feeling strange and abruptly stylish. Her cheekbones had a softer definition, owing to the little fluff of a side fringe she had been given, while the hairdresser lightly touched her ear-lobes and said affectedly that she should never hide her ears because they were one of her best features.

A grin touched Tina's lips. The vanities of high fashion and the beauty salon struck her as rather superficial and she was certain women submitted to these various tortures merely to compete with each other. She had noticed that as each customer walked out of the salon, complete with a glistening hairdo, the eyes of those awaiting their turn followed narrowly, critically. She was treated to the same examination and heard a stout, carroty woman hiss at her companion: 'That must be a new silver dye Jacques is using. I wonder if it would suit me?'

The evening before Tina and John were married, Gaye laid on a small dinner party for them. She had invited a few other friends of John's, and Tina, eager for him to be proud of her, put on one of her new dresses, a mimosa satin with a design of feather-like motifs in diamanté and sequins covering the bodice and slowly fanning into the full skirt. She dabbed mimosa perfume behind her ears, ran caressing fingers over the hoop of rubies on her left hand, then rustled into the stylish lounge of the Lannings' flat.

Chuck was still dressing, while Gaye's voice drifted in from the kitchen where she was making the sauce for the tournedos. Tina gazed around the room, hardly able to take in the fact that after tomorrow she would have an attractive home. She would arrange dinner parties, and in a bedroom next to her own *her* husband would whistle a tune to himself as he brushed his hair and put on his tie.

She wandered about the room, wrapped in pre-wedding dreams, a bud of a nerve opening and closing in the pit of her stomach. One moment she felt like laughing, the next like crying, and she almost dropped a piece of Capo di Monte pottery when the front door chimes pealed through the flat.

'I'll go,' she called through the serving-hatch, and with a fast beating heart she crossed the lounge and went out into the white-painted hallway. Behind the spotlight-glass of the front door she could see an extra tall figure, and the very lobes of her ears were rouged with her shy blush as she opened the door to John.

'You're looking very vampish this evening,' he smilingly murmured. 'I hardly recognize my Tina of the flyaway hair and the big, searching eyes.'

'Your Chorley goose is there, John, under all this fine plumage,' she replied, her hands lost in his.

This reply brought a fleeting smile of tenderness to his face and he carried her hands to his lips and gave them a light kiss.

The evening that followed was a delightful one, and all too soon it was over. John was the last guest to leave. The marriage ceremony, he reminded Tina, was arranged for eleven o'clock at the Chelsea Register Office, then after a wedding luncheon with Gaye and Chuck at Claridges, he and Tina would drive to a Surrey inn he knew of, where they would spend the night before catching their plane for Ste. Monique.

'You won't mind honeymooning on the island, and sharing me with Liza, will you, Tina?' he asked, more out of politeness than anything else, she felt.

'No,' she said, but in her heart she knew

she would have preferred to be alone for a while with John before plunging into her role of stepmother. But it couldn't be helped. The child came first with him, and she must learn to accept the fact.

John left after giving her cheek a cursory brush with his lips and she said good night to Gaye and Chuck. In the guest room she prepared for bed, tired but too tensed up for sleep, curled up on the foot of the bed and buffing her nails when the door opened to admit Gaye. She carried a beaker of Horlicks on a tray. 'This should help you sleep,' she said, flickering a look of friendly concern over Tina, who looked very young and innocent in her dolly pyjamas. 'I felt awful the night before I got married. I was suddenly certain I didn't love Chuck and I wanted to call the whole thing off. Here, drink this while it's nice and hot.'

Tina sipped at the milky drink, feeling it go down painfully over the foolish lump in her throat. So other girls spent this particular night in a state of panic, certain they were heading for disaster, and compiling a list of reasons why it might be better if they called the whole thing off . . .

Gaye sat down on the bed and pulled her pastel-flowered wrap over her legs. 'Are the butterflies settling down?' she smiled.

Tina nodded. 'Thanks for coming in like this,' she said. 'I was beginning to panic.'

'Well, it's a natural reaction, Tina. A girl doesn't get married but once in a lifetime, in normal circumstances, and loving a man is very different from living with him. I always think the courtship is the nicest part of the love game, from a girl's point of view, and you haven't had a lot of time in which to get to know John. But take it from me he's a grand person.'

Loving a man, and living with him, were two very different things, Tina reflected, but there was something she could be thankful about. Being a widower for eight years might have saddened John, even made him cynical, but he hadn't turned into one of those stony misogynists. Beneath his air of worldly assurance and occasional aloofness, she had glimpsed a man who needed to be loved. A new, anticipatory thrill ran through her. Out of the strange beginning of their marriage there might emerge something of worth . . . a child, perhaps.

She would like a child of her own. All that she had missed in her own childhood would be lavished on her daughter, or her son. Laughter, understanding, tons of love.

Gaye touched her arm. 'Don't be afraid of not measuring up to Joanna,' she said gently. 'When a woman is exceptionally good-looking, she wants a man for his worship rather than his warmth. She likes to be put on a pedestal, and it can't be exactly comfortable, living on a pedestal.'

Tina broke into a smile. 'I'm glad I was able to stay here with you, Gaye,' she said gratefully. 'I feel much better about things now.'

'Good.' Gaye leant forward and kissed her cheek. 'Now you must get some shut-eye. We don't want the bride yawning through her marriage ceremony tomorrow.'

A few minutes later Gaye had returned to her own bedroom, and Tina lay in the darkness, listening to the whisper tick of the bedside clock until it lulled her off to sleep.

She was given breakfast in bed the following morning, coffee, scrambled eggs and bacon, then cherry waffles, and all too soon it seemed it was time for her to dress for her wedding. Gaye insisted on a spot of glamour and seating Tina at the dressing-table she applied a cool rose foundation to her face, a hint of turquoise eye-shadow, and pink-ice lipstick. They were in the middle of these beauty preparations when the door chimes sounded and Chuck, a minute or so later, put his head round the bedroom door. He was grinning broadly.

'A package for the bride has just arrived,' he announced. 'Shall I toss it in?'

'Of course, you big lug.' Gaye shook her head at him. 'And don't toss it, it might be breakable.'

'I doubt that,' he chuckled. He went away, to return carrying a long white box with the famous name of Woolf stamped across it. Tina turned from the dressing-table, her heart thumping with excitement.

'You open it for me, Gaye,' she begged. 'I've got the shakes.'

Gaye obligingly slipped the ribbon and lifted the lid. She opened folds of tissue-paper, then gave a whistle of delight and lifted into the open a supple, beige-honey mink coat. A card fell from one of the wide sleeves, and Tina's hand shook as Chuck picked it up and handed it to her.

On the card was slashed darkly: 'Happy wedding day, Tina. John.'

'The coat's from John,' Tina breathed, sudden tears clinging to her lashes. 'Isn't it beautiful!'

She hugged the coat to her, her face in the soft fur, love for John almost bursting the seams of her hungry young heart. 'Oh, he shouldn't have done it! But isn't it gorgeous! A mink coat, for *me*.'

Gaye shot a smile at her husband. 'Well, you can't stand there all day cuddling it, Tina,' she said. 'If I don't get you dressed, you'll be keeping your bridegroom waiting on the register office steps.'

Chuck said he reckoned the wait would be worthwhile, and as he made his exit he lowered Tina a meaning wink. Confidence spilled through her in a warm wave. The sun was shining. John had given her a mink coat, the traditional gift of a lover, and he wished her happiness on her wedding day. She smiled into the mirror at Gaye, who was working on her hair, and closed her mind to what her husband-to-be had omitted to add on the card—his love.

She was finally in her bridal array, a borrowed lace hankie from Gaye in her handbag, John's butterfly brooch pinned to her suit lapel, both blue and no longer new, and her glistening wedding gift over her arm as she made her way into the lounge.

Gaye's husband rose smiling from the settee and tossed aside a newspaper. He walked over and took a long look at Tina, then his fingers went to his tie, the Englishman's involuntary compliment.

'Will I do?' Tina gave him a shaky smile.

'I should say so!' Chuck, like most Englishmen when they're moved, gave a hearty laugh. 'John's a lucky old sea-dog.'

Gaye came into the lounge, pulling on her gloves and breathlessly remarking that they had better be on their way. She wore a smart Simone Mirman hat, a straight beige chemise dress, and the triple pearls that best suit a mature woman.

'Here—let's wait a few more minutes, old girl,' Chuck said. 'I'm expecting a caller—ah, there goes the door chimes!'

He loped out to the hallway, leaving Gaye to raise mystified eyebrows at Tina. 'What's he up to?' she murmured.

They soon found out, for when Chuck returned to the lounge he was carrying a spray of golden-yellow honeymoon roses. 'I phoned round for them, Tina.' He blushed madly as he handed her the spray. 'All the very best, old thing.'

'Oh, Chuck!' She tiptoed and left a feather of pink-ice on his cheek. 'Thank you—thank you both, for everything!'

* * *

Despite Gaye's anxiety, they arrived at the Chelsea Register Office before John. Tina had left her coat in Chuck's car, and she stood tongue-tied while they waited for John, gripping her spray of roses and feeling the thud of her heart and the fluid weakness of her knees. Then he came brushing through the door at the end of the corridor and her heart throbbed the mysterious signals of love through her blood. She wanted to run to him, but she waited, slim and demure in her blue-smoke suit and fragile rose hat.

'Hullo, my dear!' He took hold of her left hand and squeezed it reassuringly. 'How very nice you look.'

'Gaye's handiwork,' she laughed shyly.

'You've done an excellent job, Gaye.' He slanted her a smile, but Tina couldn't help noticing that as the four of them walked to the door marked Registrar, he ran a rather quizzical glance over her upswept hair and little flirt of a side-fringe. What was he thinking, that her smart hairstyle made a stranger of her?

They entered the Registrar's office and Tina felt a nerve jigging in her throat. This was it! No backing out now, no running from what she wanted yet feared, to become the wife of this tall, distinguished man in the dark suit with a cotton-fine stripe, the sun through the office windows picking out the strands of silver in his thick dark hair.

'All right, Tina?' Gaye murmured.

She nodded, but she was pale under her make-up, and her heart seemed to be thumping in every part of her.

The crisp, unemotional ceremony began, and it came to Tina that had she been marrying John in a church, wearing an orange-blossom coronet and a cloud veil over slipper-satin, it would all have seemed like a dream. But this cluttered office, worn desk, and rather crusty official were too down-to-earth to aid an illusion.

When she said her simple yes, and felt John's gold ring sliding over her knuckle, she knew she really was the second Mrs. Trecarrel. He gave her a smile, but it was Gaye who kissed her cheek and hugged her slight, trembling figure.

They signed the Register of Marriages, the official shook hands with them, then they were out in the sunshine. They drove to Claridges in Chuck's car. John had parked his in the vicinity of the hotel, already loaded up with his baggage, to which Tina's was added. 'You look as though you've got more than sixty-six pounds each,' Chuck said. 'You'll be paying over-weight on that golfing gear, Johnny.'

The name came out so naturally, flipping Tina's heart right over. She glanced at her husband for his reaction, but he was bent imperturbably over the boot of his car, stacking Tina's new cream and blue luggage on top of his own well-used coach-hide cases with their bright spattering of travel labels. He slanted a smile at his friend. 'Couldn't resist treating myself while I was in England, Chuck. You can't buy gear like that back on the island—now is that everything, Tina? You haven't left anything in Chuck's car?'

She shook her head, feeling the first strange thrill at being treated with proprietorship by John. After he had locked the boot, then the other doors, he dropped her mink coat round her shoulders and lightly held her arm as the four of them walked into the hotel.

A delicious wedding lunch had been laid on for them, with white flowers on the table, a vintage champagne, and quiet, charming service with a smile for the bride and bridegroom. There was even a small iced cake with silver shoes on it, one of which found its way into Tina's handbag—for luck.

Chuck lifted his champagne glass towards the end of the meal and said with sincerity: 'Here's all the very best to both of you. If your partnership turns out as happy as Gaye's and mine, then you won't have much to grumble about.'

Tina and John looked at each other. For a long moment—during which she held her breath—his face was still and unreadable, then lines fanned beside his eyes and he was giving her the smile that had won her heart up on the headland at Chorley.

'I'll try not to make Tina regret our partnership,' he said.

You could never make me regret my love for you, she wanted to reply. But John had not asked for her love. He wanted only her tolerance and companionship; in exchange he was giving her a home of her own . . . a journey over the horizon she used to watch so longingly.

A quarter of an hour later they had said good-bye to Gaye and Chuck and were heading out of London. Tina, pleasantly drowsy from the champagne, snuggled down into the softness of her mink coat and watched the rows of shops slowly merge into streets of houses, then the houses became more spaced out and there were fields, road hoardings and factory sites. She had not, after all, been part of the big city for long.

'Did you write to tell your aunt about your marriage?' John asked suddenly.

'No, she wouldn't have been interested,' Tina replied, catching her lip between her teeth at the bleak remembrance of her good-bye to Aunt Maud.

'Poor little Tina,' John shot her a look that was both shrewd and tender, 'robbed of a lighthearted childhood, and now an orange-blossom wedding.'

'I didn't want orange-blossom,' she protested.

'Nor an organ playing *Oh Perfect Love*?' he drawled.

'N-no.' She glanced away from him, bathed in the heat of youthful confusion. Had he guessed how she felt about him? Was he mocking her? His funny, shy little bride . . . who mustn't take too seriously the role he meant her to play in his life?

A minute or so later the car suddenly coasted on to a lay-by and sighed to a standstill. John turned to look at her, an arm resting on the steering-wheel. 'This is our first real moment alone for several days,' he said. 'Do you feel strange, Tina? Or hasn't it hit home to you yet that you're a bride?'

A bride ... with all its implications, added the silence that followed his words.

She gazed wordlessly back at him, her eyes the colour of shaded hyacinths, her mouth innocently pink because she had forgotten to replace her lipstick after their lunch at Claridges, her little model hat no longer centrally placed on her upswept hair.

'Oh, let's take off that ridiculous thing!' Laughingly he moved closer to her and searched for the pin that secured her hat. On to the back seat flew hat and pearl-tipped pin, then with a grin cutting the edge of his mouth he withdrew the clips from her up-sweep and released her hair in a white-gold mist to her shoulders. His fingers touched it, then he drew her against his chest and laid his lips to the throb of an artery in the soft pool of her throat. It was a gentle but searching kiss, his lips tracing the artery's movement round to the silky curve of her neck. When he lifted his head, his eyes were lazy in their regard.

'Still nervous of me, Tina?' he murmured.

The soft collar of her coat framed her triangular face, with the wide eyes that knew so little of men and their passions. 'Not of you—a little of myself. I-I've never had a boy-friend, you see—' Colour stormed into her cheeks. 'I don't know what a girl does to—to—'

'Please a man?' he inquired gently. 'What do you feel like doing right now? Lovemaking is an instinct, Tina, so just follow it.'

Unsure but eager to please him, she lifted her hands to his lean, quizzical face and shyly touched the dented chin, angular jaw and silvery temples. Her fingers stroked the silvery wings and she loved the air of distinction they gave him.

He evidently assumed something quite different, for he said wryly: 'Are you realizing the big gap between our ages? Does it worry you that I have grey hairs, Tina?'

She shook her head and softly quoted Thackeray to him. 'No lace as handsome as silver hair.'

An expression of quick tenderness filled John's blue eyes. 'You're really rather charming, aren't you, my child?' His lips brushed her pink cheek. 'Perhaps I should have left you wrapped in your chrysalis until some equally charming young man came along to awaken you—'

'I don't like young men,' she protested quickly. 'I like your—your kindness and goodness to me.'

'Don't run away with the idea that I've married you out of a sense of kindness, Tina.' He turned from her and started the car. 'It's a wife I want, not a little girl to dandle on my knee. You understand me, I hope?'

'Of course, John.'

He shot a look at her. She sat holding in her lap the golden honeymoon roses Chuck had given her, an air of meek acceptance about her that drew John's brows together in a sudden harsh frown. They drove on to the inn in silence, a picturesque place nestling in a fold of the Surrey hills. They were shown to their adjoining rooms by the proprietor. Tina ran her glance round her charming bedroom. Oak furniture glimmered in its odd angles, the bed was a half-tester with a cretonne canopy and a floor-touching counterpane edged with a bobble fringe. The wood floor was scattered with tufted wool rugs, and through the tiny, chintz-hung casements there drifted the lovely scents of a country garden.

'This is your room, sir.' The inn proprietor unlocked an adjoining door. 'Dinner is at half past seven . . . we're early nighters in the country.'

He slanted the edge of a grin at Tina, then after laying the keys on the dressing-chest, he left them alone.

As they were staying only one night, John had brought up their smaller cases and after dumping Tina's on the foot of the bed he sauntered into his own room, calling back over his shoulder, 'We could go for a stroll before dressing for dinner. Would you like that?'

She caught that note of indulgence in his voice and felt her lips forming into a smile. 'Yes, I'd love it,' she called back.

'Okay. Just let me find my pipe and tobacco.'

She listened to him sorting about in his case and whistling what she vaguely recognized as a calypso. He was looking forward to returning to the island, she reflected, as she secured her hair in an Alice band. Through the mirror, as she lifted her hands, she saw the glint of her gold wedding ring and the soft red glow of her other ring. She was a wife! How strange it felt, to see a tall man walking into her bedroom and to know he had every right to be there.

'Ready?' he queried, tucking his briar into a corner of his mouth and holding out a hand to her. They ran down the stairs and as they passed the reception desk the clerk lifted his glance from what looked like a racing-form and gave them a stare. They intruded on the afternoon drowsiness that lay over the inn, and a curtain fluttered at the lounge window as they walked past on their way to the roadway. Tina glanced back and saw a woman at the window. Her eyes were avidly curious. Was she guessing that they were a honeymoon couple?

They took a random path, where the strawberry-cream of hawthorn frothed on the hedges and honeysuckle twined. A big russet butterfly flitted ahead of them, fairy light on the warm air, which was filled with the scent of cut corn in the nearby fields. Catkins hung on the hazels, while the horse-chestnuts still carried their ruby and ivory candles.

They came to a woodland, where bluebells lingered in company with brimstone cowslips and silvery drifting lady's smock. Also, beneath a copper beech, a little patch of lilies of the valley nodded their delicate bells. A cuckoo called. This, Tina thought, was England at her happiest. This woodland was a place she would remember in the weeks to come, when she was living on the sub-tropical island of Ste. Monique.

John lifted her into the fork of a tree, then while he packed his pipe and lit up, he surveyed the youthful picture his bride made with her Alice-banded fair hair, hands folded in her blue lap, and slender legs lightly swinging ... as though to music she alone could hear. 'You look at this moment like a Kate Greenaway illustration,' he remarked. 'Everyone's going to say I've robbed the schoolroom.'

'Do you mind if they say that?' she inquired, fully aware that she didn't look her age and people might remark that she wasn't much older than his daughter.

'Not particularly,' he drawled. 'Gossip can be irritating, but it's rarely lethal.'

Tina plucked a leaf and pretended to examine it. Though he said that gossip wasn't lethal, there had been some talk about him and Joanna's cousin. Had Joanna, that tragic day eight years ago, fallen into the sea with doubt and unhappiness clouding her mind and making her less careful than she would otherwise have been on her friends' yacht?

'Does it worry you, Tina, that people are going to refer to us as mutton and lamb?'

He was grinning lopsidedly as she glanced up, the shredded leaf falling from her fingers. 'I'm only worried about Liza's reaction,' she said, which was partly true. 'It's important to a second marriage that the children aren't resentful, and I've not had a chance to get to know Liza before partially taking her father away from her.'

'Children are adaptable creatures, Tina. My Liza needs a mother, someone she can confide in as she can't in a father, and in choosing to marry you I was also thinking of her. As a motherless child yourself, you already have a sympathy for others in a similar position. You know what it feels like to be without the affection only a mother can give. It's a bond Liza will be aware of herself, for she's an intelligent young thing.'

'If she's like you, John, then I'm sure I shall—get along with her.' Tina only just bit back the word love. She didn't wish to foist her deeper feelings upon him, not when he told her so frankly that his choice of a wife had been motivated by his concern for Liza.

Shadows were pointing towards the sun when they made their way back to the inn, delightfully rural with its mullioned windows and gables. 'We ought to have taken a snap of our—our honeymoon inn,' Tina said, stumbling a bit over the operative word, honeymoon.

'You can do it in the morning if you want to, you absurd young thing,' John said, knocking out his pipe against an oak tree. She flushed at the glint of mockery in his eyes, and he added: 'Don't be on the defensive with me, Tina. I'm not expecting the allure of a sophisticated woman in a girl with your kind of upbringing. Innocence has its own kind of allure, if you must know.'

'I want to be a wife you'll not be disappointed in,' she replied, tugging at a lock of her hair in a young, nervous way.

'Marriage, as I told you once before, is a

gamble for both sexes.' He pulled her fingers away from her hair and shook them. 'We may both be disappointed by this leap into the dark we're taking together.'

Pain jabbed her heart. Was he thinking of Joanna and the joy they had shared? Was he facing up to the fact that it mightn't be recaptured with anyone else? They entered the inn to the hum of evening activity. There was a sound of cutlery being laid in the dining-room and a smell of cooking wafted into the lobby as a waitress brushed through a baize door carrying rolls in a circular basket.

'Good evening, sir.' She smiled respectfully at John, but when she greeted Tina there was an inquisitive gleam in her eyes. As Tina mounted the stairs she wondered if the waitress was thinking it strange so distinguished a man should have married a girl who was neither pretty or self-assured. On the other hand she could be thinking it romantic, like a story or a film?

* * *

Tina dressed for dinner in a fondant-pink chiffon with a dove-grey sash—a romantic concoction which Gaye had suggested she dine in this particular evening.

'Don't believe that honeymoon nerves are confined to us,' she said. 'Men are often as jittery, even the most sophisticated types, and it doesn't hurt to soften them up with a girly dress.'

It also occurred to Tina to leave her hair as John seemed to prefer it, brushed until it shone and latched at the nape of her neck with a mock tortoiseshell slide, shaped like a fan, which she had brought to London from Chorley, and which she had been wearing the evening John had proposed to her. She then applied a little lipstick and decided she looked cool and fresh if no raving beauty.

She was leaning from one of the casements, breathing the dew on the grass and the vanilla scent of heliotrope, when John came in from the adjoining room. She had heard his tap on the door, but she didn't turn round. She willed him to come and stand close to her, to breathe the perfume she had dabbed behind her ears, and to maybe put his arms around her for a moment.

'Don't you want any dinner?' he said dryly. 'Personally I'm starving.'

She forced back a sigh, and when she turned round, he was holding open the door of her room and waiting for her to go down with him.

They were a trifle late making their entrance into the dining-room and speculative glances dwelt on them as they followed a waiter to their table. A woman caught Tina's eyes and beamed at her, then in the over-loud voice of the elderly she said to her dining companion: 'Those two are new—father and daughter on holiday together, I shouldn't wonder.'

Tina wanted the floor to open and swallow her, and when she finally dared a glance at John his lean face had taken on that rather forbidding expression. His dark brows were drawn together so that his eyes lay in their shadow, and the compression of his lips had hardened his jawline.

They ate in silence, Tina too miserable to appreciate the meal, while John was satisfying his hunger in an automatic fashion, broodingly working his way through smoked trout, then baked ham salad. He declined a sweet in favour of cheese, but when Tina would have followed suit, he said in a rather curt voice: 'I don't often eat dessert, Tina, but you young things like sweet concoctions. Have the chocolate soufflé if you don't fancy the pears in cider.'

Too nervous to defy him in his present mood, she asked the waiter to bring her a small portion of the soufflé, then she sat looking round the dining-room with forced interest. 'I love old oaken beams, don't you?' she said brightly. 'And those drinking horns above the fireplace must be terribly old.'

'I quite appreciate your predilection for ancient objects,' he drawled. 'It would seem that you lived too long with a much older person and that in agreeing to marry me you were only conforming to habit.' His eyes brooded on her startled face. 'What do you expect of me, I wonder, Tina? Is it a guardian . . . or is it a husband?'

Before she could reply to him, before she could assure him that she wanted him in whatever capacity he chose to want her, the waiter reappeared at the table with her sweet, and John's Camembert. John told him they would have their coffee in the lounge, where a little to Tina's relief John fell into conversation with one of the other guests, leaving her to sit quietly in the corner of a settee with a copy of *The Tatler*.

She read an article without taking in a word of it, and John eventually remarked that she could go to bed if she liked, he was going to have a pipe and a stroll before turning in.

She rose from the settee, confused and uncertain. This was their wedding night, yet there wasn't a hint of warmth or expectancy in his manner. 'I-I am a little tired,' she blurted. 'Shall I—see you later?'

His blue glance ran over her young troubled face, and as she steeled herself to meet his rejection she put back her shoulders and tilted her chin. John narrowed his eyes as he watched her do this, then with a hint of impatience in his voice, he said: 'If you're asleep when I come up I shan't disturb you.'

'All right.' She turned from him and made for the door, feeling in her pretty chiffon dress not unlike a child who had dressed for a party which had not taken place.

'Off to bed, my dear?' said a voice.

Tina saw that she was being addressed by the woman who had made that over-loud remark in the dining-room. With gregarious friendliness she went on to ask how long Tina was staying here.

'My husband and I leave in the morning,' Tina replied, adding a quick good night before the woman could give voice to any more tactless remarks.

A few minutes later she was alone in her bedroom, gazing into the mirror at her pathetic finery. Lord, how young and naïve she looked! That was how John saw her. No wonder he was hardly interested in following her up to bed.

She went to one of the casements, but the garden was dark and the scent of the nicotiana rich and fragrant. She couldn't see John, she only felt bleakly that some of the enchantment of her wedding day had dissolved and would not return. She lifted her hands and pressed them to her cold face, for here she was, no longer living a dream, but tied to a stranger whose moods were already beginning to baffle her.

'I can be kind—but I can also be cruel,' he had warned her. It seemed that he had not warned her in vain.

She unlatched her suitcase and took out her night-dress and negligée. Rows of frilled lace curved round the yokes of the delicate matching garments, and as she laid them on the bed she reflected wryly that she might as well have packed an unromantic pair of pyjamas. From John's attitude downstairs, one might assume that he wouldn't care much if she was fast asleep when he came to bed.

She prepared for bed, then clad in her honeymoon finery she slipped between crisp sheets redolent of lavender. She tucked the pillow into a mound under her cheek, and though she didn't mean to fall asleep, her day had been a full one and she was emotionally disturbed as well. The dream she drifted into was about Chorley and Aunt Maud. But in her dream her aunt was kind and understanding and that old house on Dulcey Avenue was alive with friends. It was all as pleasant as the reality had been grim, and Tina woke up just as she was on the point of blowing out the candles on the twenty-first birthday cake she had not really had.

'Now you must blow out all the candles,' everyone at the party was saying. 'If you don't, your dreams won't come true . . .'

The dream fled away. Tina sat up with a start, John's name breaking from her lips.

He came to the door of the adjoining room. He had removed his jacket and tie and his white shirt lay open at his throat His hair where he had been walking alone in the night breezes was ruffled—making him shatteringly attractive to the girl who sat gazing at him with big, sleep-misted eyes.

'Go back to sleep, honey,' he said gently. 'You've had a long day, and tomorrow we'll be doing a lot of travelling.'

Though he used that little endearment, it was as though he spoke to a child—to Liza! But Tina wasn't a child. She was his wife ... and she wanted her dreams to come true, not to flicker dangerously in the draught of other people's unthinking remarks.

She threw back her bedcovers as he strolled back into his own room. She pattered after him in bare feet. 'John, don't treat me like a child,' she said. 'Coming here in the car you—you were different.'

His glance flickered over her. The fine silk of her shell-pink nightdress hung softly about the slight contours of her body, her ashen hair glimmered about her pale, upraised face. On the hand that caught at his cuff there shone the gold and ruby symbols of his ownership.

'I'm prepared to be a wife to you,' she said shyly. 'I want to help you forget—'

'Forget what?' The words leapt at her.

'You—you know,' she faltered.

'My first marriage?' he baited her cruelly. 'Is that what you're referring to?'

At once she let go of his cuff and backed away from him. His eyes were suddenly shimmering—she had probed his secret wound and in his pain he looked a harsh-faced stranger who might be capable of anything.

'Talking about my first marriage doesn't come easy to me, Tina,' his hands caught at her shoulders and his fingers bit into the fine bones as though he needed to inflict pain in order to ease his own, 'and you might as well know now, as later, that I have no intention of dredging to the surface things that are best left hidden. Out of sight they don't hurt quite so much, but as for forgetting them—' his harsh glance swept over her face, 'I doubt whether that possibility exists.'

'I-I'm so sorry, John.' The words were inadequate, but her sensitive pride had crept back into its shell and she could not offer him her love. She could not say that she wanted him despite everything. She shivered as he released her and felt the ache where his fingers had gripped her.

'Go back to bed, Tina,' he said. 'You're

looking whacked.'

'John—' she stood before him, nervously twisting her rings, 'you aren't regretting our marriage, are you?'

'I think it might be a good idea if we got to know each other a little better.' He narrowed his eyes. 'You'd prefer that, wouldn't you?'

She knew it was what he wanted, so she nodded her head.

'Come along, I'll tuck you up.' He scooped her up in his arms and carried her to her bed. He tucked the bedclothes in and brushed the flyaway hair from her eyes. 'Sleep tight, my dear. We've a long day ahead of us tomorrow.'

She lay there looking at him, and with a smile he bent and lightly kissed her mouth. The door closed behind him. And so ended Tina's wedding day.

CHAPTER FOUR

THERE was a faint humming in Tina's ears, while she experienced the oddest sensation whenever she realized that beneath the floor on which her feet rested there was an immensity of space and nothing else.

She gazed out of the window beside her and saw the sky all around them. The jumbo jet, like a huge fly on the ceiling of heaven, buzzed with regular monotony as it bore her to her new home. John's newspaper no longer rustled as he turned the pages, so she knew he was staring in front of him and thinking about the island. Visualizing all that was beloved and familiar—and painful to him. She bit her lip and wished their first night together had turned out differently. Some of the barriers between them would have been down and she could have slipped an arm through his and felt much more of a real wife . . .

'Feeling nervous, Tina?' John put a hand over hers and pressed it. When she looked at him there was a disturbing quality about his smile that got right to her; a hint of sadness, she thought, and her fingers twisted beneath his to interlace with their hard leanness.

'A little,' she admitted, which was definitely an understatement. Her knees were literally knocking.

'You'll soon get the hang of things,' he reassured her. His sea-blue glance searched out the apprehension in her young face. 'I doubt whether Liza will be very bashful with you, if that's what you're worried about. When she sees how youthful you are she'll probably regard you as her own special playmate, brought all the way from England by her doting father.'

Beneath his bantering tone there lurked a shade of seriousness, and Tina knew, with a jolting heart, that John was questioning the wisdom of their marriage—all because that darned woman at the inn had referred to them as father and daughter. Tina wanted to say outright that she didn't feel in the least like his daughter, but this was neither the place nor the time for such a declaration. She could only hope that once they had settled down together at Blue Water House, things would work out between them. They must! He meant so very much to her—more than could ever be put into words!

'Do you fancy an appetizer before lunch?' he asked.

She nodded, and he beckoned one of the smartly uniformed hostesses and ordered a sherry for Tina and Dimple Haig with water for himself. While they enjoyed their drinks he talked about the island, describing the tranquillity of its lagoons where coral scattered the sands like broken flowers, but where stingrays might also lurk, and the sea hide giant squids and saw-toothed barracuda in its turquoise depths . . .

The rest of his drink was abruptly gone from his glass and Tina saw his glance rest on his stretched-out left leg. She remembered what Gaye had told her, that in his attempt to save Joanna he had torn open his leg and been attacked by a barracuda. He had almost lost his own life that tragic day—and afterwards people had gossiped about him and Joanna's cousin!

Tina launched into questions about the island in an attempt to take their minds off more personal matters, and she seemed to succeed, for in a while John was looking much less taut and even smiling as he described the antics of some of the West Indians he had working for him. Tina hadn't known until now that her husband owned a citrus plantation. It was fairly large and managed, he told her, by a cousin-in-law named Ralph Carrish.

'The house and the plantation were left to me by a bachelor uncle,' John added. 'The Trecarrels have always had roving blood in them, and many years ago one of them was an officer on the ship that discovered Ste. Monique. He settled down on the island as a planter, raised a family, which gradually dwindled down to this uncle of mine. Upon his death I took over the house and the estate. I—work on the island, which is one of the reasons I've never left it. Ralph is a thoroughly reliable manager, so I've no worries on that score.'

John's eyes met Tina's. 'Ralph and my first wife were cousins. He has a sister, Paula, whom you will meet. She runs his bungalow for him. It isn't, by the way, anything like an English bungalow. It's quite large, very picturesque. Paula is an artistic creature and she's turned the place into quite an eyeful. You'll get on well with Ralph, I should think.'

Which remark, Tina reflected, could mean that she might not get on with Paula. Somehow Tina didn't expect to. If Paula wanted John, she wasn't going to be overjoyed to meet his new wife!

They had lunch. Tiny, delicious Trinidad oysters, aspic chicken with a green salad, followed by sliced mangoes in dry champagne. Tina had a good meal. Afterwards John remarked: 'I'm glad I haven't landed myself with a sickly travelling companion, grabbing at paper bags all the time. That would have been fun.'

'I'm pleased with myself,' Tina smiled back. 'I was awfully worried in case I had air-sickness. I mean, I've done so little travelling.'

'What about summer holidays?' John inquired.

'Well, we lived near the sea and Aunt Maud saw no point in going away.'

'You haven't played at all, have you, Tina?' He spoke gently. 'Well, we must remedy that on the island. You'll be able to swim, explore, play tennis. I'll teach you to ride as well, and drive. We've a speed limit, which is a good thing, for no one need go at the pace some people go it back in England. They'll lose the ability to enjoy simple pleasures if they're not careful.'

'Is that one of the reasons why you prefer to live on an island?' Tina asked.

'One of them,' John agreed, watching as she flipped open a pancake-compact and dabbed at her nose with a penny-sized puff. She noticed in the small mirror the petals of colour which his lazy scrutiny brought to her cheeks. She wondered—uncontrollably—if he was comparing her to

Joanna, and quickly shut the compact and slipped it into her bag. She wasn't vain. She knew that her pretensions to good looks were limited to a clear skin and a certain luminosity about her eyes.

'No lipstick?' he drawled amusedly.

'Do you—want me to wear it?' She gave him a shy, uncertain glance.

'You must please yourself about such things, Tina.' His amusement was faintly touched with surprise at her question. 'Do I strike you as a tyrant?'

'Of course not!' she exclaimed. 'But you may be one of those men who dislike cosmetics.'

This remark underlined the little she really knew about him and his tastes, and somewhat quizzically he said: 'I can take them in small doses, but I do happen to think that they're less attractive on young things like yourself. It isn't that older women always need the embellishment, but they carry it off with a certain admirable panache.'

'I wish I were a little older,' Tina sighed, knowing she'd have more assurance and not be reduced to a bundle of nerves at the thought of being châtelaine of Blue Water House and stepmother to another woman's child.

'Quit worrying and take things as they come,' John advised, blowing out the flame of the match he applied to a narrow cheroot and putting his seat into a reclining position. He lay smoking with an air of contentment that warmed Tina's heart. He was right, of course, she must take things as they came. Not give way to youthful impetuosity to have everything at once—especially his love.

They still had about three hours' flight ahead of them, and Tina dozed off, awakening suddenly to find the lights on in the cabin and darkness beyond the windows. John told her they were approaching the island of Jamaica, where his motor-launch would be waiting to take them across to Ste. Monique. The various landing signs flashed on, and because Tina's hands were shaky, John fastened her seat belt for her.

Now the big plane was dropping like a bird through the air and very gradually there was a speckling of lights far below them. A wavy necklet where the harbour humped out into the sea, straightening out into the sweep of Kingston, scattering up the hillsides where habitations were dotted.

The sea was dense as velvet, with a lighthouse thrusting out of it like a stick of rock. Mountains showed against the star-glow, and Tina could feel her heart performing excitable little somersaults, her fingers gripping her husband's unaware as the landing gear and brake flaps vibrated. The plane skimmed at a tremendous rate along a runway of the terminal, then came twin thumps, a gradual lessening of speed and beyond the cabin windows the brightly lit airport buildings.

Passengers were requested to remain seated while the aircraft was cleared by the Health Authorities, then they were outside in the warm evening air, tinged by a spiciness that flickered Tina's nostrils and creaking with the antics of hidden crickets.

The ensuing three-quarters of an hour was a mill of people, voices, chocolate-coloured officials looking at various certificates, and finally a pink-palmed hand chalking on their baggage and releasing them into the velvety dusk. Beyond the barrier John spotted a couple of men who were obviously waiting to act as porters, and within seconds he had obtained their services. Their high, sing-song voices intrigued Tina as they carried the various suitcases to a taxi. Tina and John squeezed in, then with its headlamps full on the vehicle zoomed in the direction of Kingston harbour, where lights spangled the various sea craft, and a big, genial islander awaited them, a yachting cap pushed to the back of his crinkly head and a wide, shy, friendly grin showing his white teeth.

'This is my wife, Joe,' John said, while Tina shivered a little at his side, not with cold but with excitement and apprehension.

'I'm glad to know you, ma'am.' Joe touched his cap and towered over her, a gentle giant she couldn't help liking the look of. 'I hope you'll be mighty happy.'

'How's Liza?' John wanted to know.

'The little missy is fine, boss. And sure keen to see you home agin. She been jumpin' like a jelly-bean all dis day and there ain't been no holdin' her.'

John laughed, and as though he had to communicate his eagerness to see his daughter he hooked an arm about Tina and gave her a brief hug.

The motor-launch was attached by a rope to a bollard, and boards sounding under John's feet as he leapt to them and held out his hands to Tina. He swung her with ease to his side, then he proceeded to stack their baggage as Joe handed it down to him. At last they were ready to set off for home. The launch quivered as the engine leapt to life, and as Joe steered her away from the dock he looked enormous, outlined against the starlight.

Tina stood alone by the rail as her husband talked to Joe, the sea breezes catching at the ends of her hair and whipping them back from her neck. Overhead the Milky Way was a scarf of glittering sequins, and as Kingston fell away and was lost to sight, the purr of the motor and the burr of deep male voices brought to Tina a transient sense of peace. She was on the last lap of her journey to her new home. *Her* home. Blue Water House. The dream place she had never expected to see, let alone live in. Her hands locked about the rail in front of her. Less than a fortnight ago she had been travelling from Chorley to London, with no thought in her mind beyond finding herself digs and a job. That was all she had visualized for Tina Manson, the shy young typist who had finally broken the tyranny of a loveless relationship.

Yet now, right this moment, she was on

board a motor-launch that was skimming through Caribbean waters. Furthermore she was married to a charming, disturbing, haunted stranger, embroiled again in a relationship that could prove heartbreaking for her.

* * *

The journey to the island took several hours, and John's cook had packed a food hamper for them. They picnicked on deck, eating steak sandwiches washed down by the best coffee Tina had ever tasted.

'It's crushed from Blue Mountain berries,' John told her, refilling the cup she held out to him.

'It's heavenly coffee.' She held both hands round the cup as she sipped at it. The sweet, strange intimacy of this alfresco meal was something she was locking away in her memory. Right now John was exclusively hers, but too soon would she be sharing him with other people. People who might resent her. Liza, for instance! For eight years her father had belonged solely to her, now she was going to have to share him—with a woman who was a total stranger. A woman he might not love, but one who was his wife, to whom in propinquity he would be bound to turn for the intimacies he was entitled to. Tina gave a little shiver at the thought. He had gone to the rail and he stood there tall, bold-featured, the tropical breezes ruffling his hair. The darkness hid the lines in his face and the silver in his hair. As he stood there, half turned away, he might have been again the young husband of Joanna.

As he stood there, his gaze on the water, was he thinking of Joanna? Must it always be like that—even when he held her in his arms—his thoughts and his heart for Joanna?

He took out his pipe and his tobacco-pouch, and when in a while the strong but fragrant whorls of smoke came to Tina, she rose and joined him at the rail—for this was *her* John. The jutting pipe, the crinkly smile—these were *hers*.

'The sea smells good,' he murmured. 'Do you like it?'

'Mmmm,' she nodded. 'Are the tropical nights always this balmy?'

'A good deal of the time.' Casually he hooked her to his side, unknowing that in doing so he made the evening heavenly for her. 'Some shattering storms do blow up at times, then towards August we have to expect a hurricane or two. But on the whole Ste. Monique is quite a paradise. You're going to like it there. I knew you would back in England, that afternoon on the cliff. Do you remember?'

She smiled to herself. Would she ever be likely to forget? 'Yes, I remember,' she said softly. 'When you told me about Ste. Monique I fell in love with it then and there.'

As though the word 'love' intrigued him, he slanted her a downward glance. 'You asked me last night, Tina, if I had any regrets regarding our marriage. Have you any?' He hesitated. 'I mean, you're young and presumably of a romantic disposition—it would be understandable if you missed being romantically wooed before being won.'

'I'm quite satisfied with things as they are,' she assured him. 'I wanted to marry you—'

'Obviously out of loneliness.' There was an understanding tone to his voice. 'That is the one big thing we have in common. I wonder if it will lead to other, bigger things? Not right now, but eventually, when we've grown more used to each other.

Do you think it possible?'

She hoped, fervently, that it was possible.

'This is how I see the situation,' he went on. 'We'll regard ourselves more or less as an engaged couple and progress towards a deeper relationship, at a pace that need not frighten you. You were frightened last night, weren't you? You looked at me—when I suggested you go to bed—like a gallant little soldier bracing yourself to leave your bunk hole for no-man's-land. You tilted your chin, put back your shoulders—my poor child, I knew exactly how you were feeling!'

No! Oh, no! The denial cried through her. I love you—I wanted you—

He took her by the shoulders as she tensed to give voice to her feelings. He added, in a hardening tone: 'We won't discuss the matter any more. Let things take their course, but if the situation doesn't work out between us—well, there's a remedy.'

A remedy! An annulment, a putting right of the mistake he might have made in marrrying her? The voice of her clamouring love was stifled. It sank mute within her. John thought she had married him for the same reason he had married her, and it could only embarrass him and confuse the issue to reveal that she loved him. He was a man of integrity and he would hate hurting her with his lesser feelings. As it was he thought they could build up a workable relationship based on mutual respect and need . . . he wouldn't say that love had died in him the day Joanna's lifeless body had been brought out of the sea. He didn't have to say it, he just hunched over the rail and seemed to forget Tina's presence.

An hour later they came in sight of the palm trees fringing the beach below Blue Water House, and soon they were edging through a V-shaped channel in the barrier reef. The currents here were at conflict and when the launch struck into them they turned in unison to spit their white fury at its intrusive bows. The coral jagged out of the water like weird branches, but Joe, with a cool nonchalance—there are no finer seamen than these Cayman Islanders—steered a straight, true course to the wide crescent of a beach that was Trecarrel property. The engine cut out as they berthed by the jetty. John sprang out and made fast. Tina, sleepy and bemused, was helped over the side by Joe.

'You're home, missus,' he beamed.

'Welcome to Ste. Monique, Tina,' John added. Then to Joe: 'Leave the bulk of the baggage on board until the morning. Just hand me that small case of my wife's—that's the one! Thanks, Joe. Now off home with you, or I shall have Topaz scolding me in the morning.'

Joe's laughter rang out as John took Tina by the elbow and led her up the beach to a flight of steps cut into the stone of the cliffs. These were lit at intervals by battery-lamps and because the steps were shallow and wide the climb was less tedious than it might otherwise have been. They came out on a headland with a path pointing directly ahead of them. John's fingers tightened on Tina's arm.

'We're almost home,' he said. 'Soon you'll be tumbling into bed.'

She gave him a drowsy smile, relieved that they had come home at this hour, when she could escape almost at once to her room and not have to meet the members of his household just yet.

They were evidently approaching the house from the rear, for now they were walking upon stone flags through a dark garden where cicadas throbbed and tree-frogs croaked. The tropical fragrances of the plants almost stunned Tina, while great ghostly months brushed her hair, sending her closer to John.

She heard him laugh above her head. 'This is like an elopement in reverse, isn't it?' he said. 'Instead of the happy couple sloping off into the night to marry, here we are creeping in. That's what comes of marrying a bohemian sculptor, Tina.'

'I think it's rather romantic,' she murmured. 'Much more exciting than a prosaic arrival in daylight—'

'With the servants lined up to greet us, eh?' he broke in dryly.

'Yes, that too,' she admitted.

'You baby.' His voice in the darkness had a deep brown sound, so thrilling that Tina was tempted to sway against him and maybe trigger off something—anything. The moment prickled with possibilities, then was lost as lights speared the star-dusted gloom and the bulk of the house loomed into view.

If Tina had hoped to avoid meeting people tonight, she quickly learned upon entering the house that there were others who were determined to meet her, despite the lateness of the hour, chimed out by a lovely old rosewood clock. As she stood beside John in the hall, confused by its oak-lined grandeur, gracious double staircase, and arcaded niches leading to various rooms, a dignified coloured manservant murmured words of welcome then apologetically informed them that Mr. Ralph and his sister were in the salon waiting to welcome them home.

'Oh, lord!' John pushed a hand over his face. A quizzical brow arched above his left eye as he caught Tina's startled glance. 'I'm sorry, my dear, but it looks as though we have a welcoming committee after all. I can't spare you the ordeal, I'm afraid. Ralph is my closest friend. And Paula—well, it wouldn't do to antagonize your nearest feminine neighbour. Let's get it over.'

Nathaniel, the butler, went ahead of them and opened with superb dignity a pair of tall, carved doors. He then stood aside for Tina to precede her husband into the salon. She nearly tripped on the thick Turkey carpet and felt colour storm into her cheeks as she met the interested gaze of a man with a crinkly, young-old face and thinnish hair. He sat away from the wings of a big chair, then stood up with a quick smile. In another chair a pale arm stretched with a cigarette to an ash-tray on a low, carved table. On the long, beautiful hand there was a big pearl ring. Thin but shapely legs clasped in gossamer stockings were the next thing you noticed about Paula Carrish. Tina, who had never pretended to be worldly, knew instinctively that this was a curiously exciting woman who didn't need a beautiful face in order to attract men. Like her brother she abruptly stood up, rather too tall for a woman, with the hungry figure of a French mannequin, the dark fiery silk of her hair plaited into a coronet that contrasted vividly with thick creamy skin that was untouched by the sun, and long, heavy-lidded, glow-worm green eyes.

Tina thought of glow-worms because she knew they flickered green in the dark in order to attract the males! Paula Carrish's eyes had such a flicker between the long, straight lashes that had been thickly darkened with mascara.

No, not beautiful, but sensationally dangerous in her slinky femininity that must hit most men dead between the eyes!

Her gliding appraisal took in every

aspect of Tina's appearance as she stood there under the bright flow of light from one of the chandeliers. With a cruel clarity it revealed the weary crescents beneath Tina's eyes, the nervous way she clenched her bottom lip with childish teeth, the uncertainty with which she entered this great, grand house as its new mistress.

The tension was lifted slightly as the two men clasped their hands together in a hearty handshake. 'This is Tina,' John said, lightly, no underlining note or pride in his voice. 'Tina, meet Ralph, whom you'll be seeing a lot of in future.'

Her hand was gripped, hazel-green eyes smiled down warmly upon her. 'I'm glad to know you, Tina.' He spoke with genuine friendliness, a much less complicated person than his sister appeared to be.

Tina's eyes met Paula's, and she decided that this cousin of Joanna's was a remarkably good actress, for not a quiver of inward hostility was echoed in her voice or betrayed by the flicker of a mascaraed eyelash as she drawled at John: 'You sly dog! When we received your cable we half wondered if you were having us on.'

'Well, now you have the evidence to prove I wasn't.' He touched Tina's shoulder and there seemed to be an edge of derision to his smile when he suggested that Ralph pour out drinks.

'Yes, we must drink to the occasion,' Ralph agreed with enthusiasm. 'Now why couldn't I have had your luck while I was on leave? All I seemed to get tangled up with were party-type girls.'

'Bachelors are always more adept at preserving their freedom than widowers, my pet.' Paula had a seductive tendency to swallow her r's, Tina noticed, watching as John held a table-lighter to the cigarette the tapering fingers plucked out of a silver box. Then she put back her rich sienna head and let smoke trickle from her nostrils, staring all the while at John. He returned her stare, and Tina wondered in that moment what incredible motive had led him to punish Paula by marrying someone as nondescript as herself. Love had not motivated his choice. But could it be that hc was getting back at Paula ... who had been with Joanna when she had fallen over the side of that yacht.

'Sit down, Tina.' John gestured rather impatiently towards a winged chair, where she sat on the edge, her eyes dark with her disturbing thoughts. Who could tell what anyone might be capable of, in the grip of a strong love, which could also hold elements of hatred . . .

Then, catching John's frowning glance, Tina shifted into the depths of her chair and tried to relax. She was overwrought from their long journey and imagining an emotional undertow that might not exist at all. She fixed her attention on the salon, octagonal in shape with long windows under recessed, shell-edged arches, the curtains glimmering deeply blue against the honey-toned panelling. The furnishings and general set-up of the room were of the Colonial era, which nonetheless imparted an air of serenity that Tina welcomed—and needed.

'I've made it cognacs,' Ralph said, bringing over a circular tray with balloon glasses on it. When each of them held a drink, he added with deep sincerity: 'All the best, you two!'

His sister drawled: 'Here's hoping you'll both be happy!'

Tina sank her nose into her glass after a swift glance at John, who was cradling his drink in lean hands and looking enigmatical. He had heard it as well, the way Paula had stressed the word 'hoping'.

Tina was beginning to know that blank look of his, which meant he was shutting himself in with his private thoughts and feelings—shutting her out!

'You paid a visit to Devon, I suppose, John?' Paula queried.

'No, I didn't get as far as the West Country,' he replied.

'Tina speaks like a country girl,' curious green eyes flickered over her unreadable face. 'I thought perhaps—'

'Tina's from Sussex.'

'That's rather a nice part of England,' Ralph put in. 'Did you live near the sea, Tina?'

'Like in the well-known song,' Paula drawled, smiling and lounging on the arm of a chair, more openly dangerous now—perhaps because John's hair was still attractively sea-ruffled, his eyes faintly drowsy, the dark grey of his suit aiding and abetting his lean air of distinction. A man you *wanted*, Tina thought, clutched by the throat when for a moment his blue eyes dwelt on her, deep in her winged chair, moon-pale against the wine upholstery.

'Yes, I lived near the sea.' She glanced quickly away from her husband and met the quiet safety of Ralph's smile.

Expressions of mutual approval lit their eyes, and it occurred to Tina that she and this man would have made a much more satisfactory brother and sister than he and Paula made.

'Good,' he grinned. 'We must fix up a swimming date.'

'You'd bettter watch out, John,' Paula laughed silkily. 'These two appear to be forming a mutual admiration club.'

'I think I can trust Ralph,' John retorted, and then he swung to face the double doors of the salon as they burst open to admit a pyjama-clad, tousle-haired child. 'Liza!' John quickly set aside his brandy glass as the child came racing towards him. He swept her up in his arms, and Tina coveted the deep, warm note of love in his voice, the way he hugged the little girl as though he wanted to break her.

'Pops! Oh, Pops!' She nuzzled his face and wrapped her arms about his neck. 'Ooh, I've missed you!'

'I've missed you, my baby, like the very devil!' He soundly kissed his young daughter. 'You really should have been asleep hours ago, you young witch,' he crooned.

'I couldn't sleep—I've been dying to see

you! Oh, Pops,' tears thickened her voice, 'I'm so glad you're home!'

'Me too, honey: I've been longing to get back home to you, but there's been so much happening. What did you think of my news?'

She mumbled something, and with a faintly quizzical grin he turned round still holding the child. Across the room his eyes met Tina's. She had risen from her chair, feeling at a disadvantage because she had hoped to meet Liza when she and John were alone with the child. With Paula looking on, her eyes narrowed into those curious, flickering slits of green, an odd air of excitement about her as though she secretly hoped that Liza was going to be antagonistic, Tina lost her poise. She looked as shy and uncertain as the little girl, whom John now lowered to her bare feet and brought over towards his young wife.

'Well, here's my sprig, Tina,' he smiled—that endearing tinge of colour seeping under his tanned skin and getting right at Tina. Shy and uncertain as she felt, she wanted to put her arms round man and child and offer all the love she was capable of.

'Go and say hullo to Tina,' John gave Liza's shoulder an encouraging squeeze.

The child dug her toes into the carpet, then she came a step or two in Tina's direction and shyly held out her hand. 'How do you do, Miss—I mean—Tina?'

Tina quivered into a smile. Liza was leggy and thin, with straight black fringe above deep hyacinth-blue eyes. 'Mayn't I kiss you, Liza?' she asked.

It was a delicate moment, and even as a faint hiss came from Paula, a flush lit the child's rather sallow skin and she gave her cheek to Tina's kiss. Then she stepped back against John, and he, scooping her up in his arms once more, told her to say good night to everyone and carried her away to her bed.

As he carried me, last night, Tina reflected.

'It looks as though you'll get along all right with the kid,' Ralph smiled encouragingly. 'She's a nice little thing. Takes after John more than—' There he broke off and looked a trifle embarrassed.

'Oh, go on, Ralph,' Paula had turned to the glass-fronted drinks cabinet and was helping herself to another drink, 'finish what you were about to say. Liza doesn't take after Joanna. She hasn't her looks, or that highly-strung tendency to channel all her love into one direction.'

'The kid's more normal,' Ralph muttered, shooting a look that was half irritated, half worried at his sister. 'As soon as John comes back we'll be off home, I think. He and Tina have had a long day of it. They'll want to get off to bed.'

Paula stood draped against the glossy wood of the drinks cabinet, black chiffon falling back and revealing the pale cream of her arm as she raised her glass to her lips. 'I take it you didn't have much time for a honeymoon, Tina?' she said. 'Tell me, exactly how long have you known John?'

'Long enough,' Tina retorted spiritedly, a little more confident of her position here now she had met and had a minor success with Liza. The child was not going to be an additional problem, thank goodness, while Ralph Carrish was obviously on her side. He was loyal to John. He would be her friend, as well.

'We live about three miles away, Tina, and we'll look forward to a visit from you,' he said, as though picking up the thread of her thought. 'I'll show you over the plantation. I know you'll enjoy seeing how we grow the fruit and process it.'

'That's a date,' Tina smiled back, a quick gleam of interest lighting her eyes.

'It's one of the most productive plantations on the island and John nets a very nice income from it,' Paula's tones had grown edged, her glance travelled up from Tina's brand new shoes to her simple but beautifully cut suit. It was plain what her glance was hinting at, and Tina felt a sudden rush of antagonism towards this green-eyed, strangely fascinating woman. It wasn't possible that *they* could ever have been friends. It looked, instead, as though they were going to be enemies, and Tina was far from experienced in dealing with the thrusts Paula Carrish looked capable of inflicting.

It was a relief to see John striding back into the salon, a lingering smile of tenderness on his mouth. 'The young monkey's asleep at last,' he said. 'Your meeting with her went quite well, eh, Tina? A bit of luck, that.'

'Tina's very obvious youth probably helped there.' Paula drawled. Then with a bland smile she added: 'We've an interesting new addition to our island society, John. A French bachelor. Will it be all right if I bring him along for drinks one evening? He's interested in the arts.'

'By all means bring him,' John agreed. 'What's he doing on the island? Enjoying a vacation?'

'He's rich, darling. Pleases himself what he does and where he goes. Quite a character, isn't he, Ralph?'

Ralph grinned. 'I guess a female might think so. Most of you women go for husky heartbreakers, don't you?'

'Do we?' His sister flickered a look that was almost deliberate over John's lean, faintly sardonic face. 'Well, so long for now, Johnny—Tina.'

As Ralph said good night to Tina, there was a questioning look in his eyes and she guessed what was on his mind. She would have to be pretty slow not to sum up his sister's feelings for John, and Ralph, quite naturally, was disturbed by the situation. He had in fact the look of a man torn by conflicting loyalties, and Tina, whose own love was an emotion leavened by pain, gave him a steady, understanding smile.

'It's been a pleasure meeting you, Tina,' he said, then he flipped a hand in John's direction, after which Paula and he were escorted to the front door by the butler.

There was a faint roar as a sports car shot away into the night.

'Paula's at the wheel!' John's smile was tautly savage as he glanced at Tina. Then he came across to her and took her by the shoulders. 'You've made a hit with Ralph. He's a nice guy, isn't he? You and he are two of a kind.'

'Why, am I nice?' Tina's faintly shy smile slanted her cheekbones and gave her am impish look. Now she had met Paula she knew she was going to have to fight every inch of the way to keep the husband who might harbour a tormenting desire for that cream-skinned, magnetic creature. She who had stood and watched as his first wife drowned! Who had wanted him then—and who had not stopped wanting him!

'Are you trying to vamp me?' John pushed a strand of flaxen hair behind her ear and watched amusedly for her inevitable blush. When it came—darn it!—he held her to his chest and softly laughed her name against her temple. 'You're falling asleep on your feet, child. Let's go to bed!'

They crossed the hall to that grand staircase of massive oak, its newel posts capped with urns of carved flowers and vinery, and John called out to Nathaniel to lock up. They mounted the stairs and the intimacy of it was something private and lovely. She had come home, perhaps to an unsettling atmosphere, but she had courage and she had hope.

* * *

Their rooms were separated by an attractive little lounge with arched entrances at either side, screened by golden brocade drapes. Tina's overnight case had been unpacked and her nightwear was laid out on her wide divan bed, whose lavender cover flounced to the flowering lilac carpet which matched the silken sweep of the curtains. Here again the panelling was honey-hued, there were mirrored dress closets, silk-shaded lamps on amber stands, and ribbed velvet bedroom chairs. Her dressing-table was lit by gilt lamps with silk half-shades, and laid out on the plate-glass top there was her new brush and comb set, a chased silver box, presumably for her trinkets, and cut-glass sprays waiting to be filled with her favourite perfume.

The pastel loveliness of the room took her breath away. Everything was so fresh and new that she couldn't help but guess that John had wired orders, specific ones, regarding the furnishing of his bride's bedroom. As she gazed around her, she wondered if the room had once been occupied by Joanna. The colour scheme would have been different, not these pastels that suited her own fair looks, but colours more specific—perhaps exotic.

Tina prepared for bed, tired out and yet so restless that she had to go out on her balcony for a few minutes. A mass of jasmine cloaked her balcony parapet, rustling and scented. The night air was still quite warm, stirring against her bare throat, where a pulse hammered as John came out of the adjoining balcony belonging to the lounge between their rooms. The light behind him framed his dark head and square, strong shoulders under the grey silk of his robe.

'Feeling homesick for England?' he asked her gently.

'Not really. I'm just enjoying a breather before turning in. The air's intoxicating. I'm drunk with the scents—there must be a thousand of them flying about like those big moths.'

He smiled, his hands thrust into his

pockets. 'What did you think of Liza?'

'She's like you, John.' Tina's eyes could have given her away, so she directed her gaze towards the dark, cicada-haunted garden. 'Did she say anything about me?'

'She said you were little, and that you looked kind.' His voice had roughened slightly, as though he were moved to emotion by the thought of his young daughter. 'I told you, didn't I, that you'd have little trouble winning her affection?'

'It's an enormous relief,' Tina said, with a shaky laugh. 'Just think of the added complication if Liza had taken a dislike to me!'

'What do you mean exactly by "added complication", Tina?' He spoke rather sharply, and when she shot a look at him she saw that he was frowning. Panic struck through her heart. What had made her say such a thing just as John had drawn closer to her!

'I didn't mean anything specific, John.' In her distress she gripped the iron lacing of the parapet between them. 'It was just a figure of speech.'

'It was nothing of the sort,' he cut in. 'If every ravishing woman you meet out here is going to be a cause for suspicion, then we're in for a jolly time.' Suddenly he leaned closer to the parapet, his eyes stabbing blue fires at her. 'Let's get something straight, I want peace from my second marriage, not jealousy and scenes. Sleep on it, eh?'

She nodded dumbly, and watched him swing on his heel and disappear through the french windows of the lounge. The light plunged out, and shivering now in the warm, scented darkness Tina groped with the curtains of her room and let them fall into place behind her, shutting out the starlight. Her heart felt banded by pain. It wasn't enough to love someone. You had to trust them, and the atmosphere there had been between John and Paula Carrish did not make for a feeling of trust.

CHAPTER FIVE

TINA awoke to dazzling sunshine and the beaming, coffee-coloured face of a trimly uniformed maid who was holding a tray with tea things on it.

'I'm Topaz, ma'am.' Splendid teeth sparkled, matching the bluey whites of the coloured woman's eyes. 'Mr. John, he give orders for you to have tea, an' he say he join you for breakfast after he take his mornin' swim.'

Topaz had looped back the mosquito netting and Tina sat up, pushing the tumbling hair away from her eyes, the sun glistening on it and bringing a rather awed look into the maid's eyes as she settled the teatray across Tina's lap. It stood on little legs and was attractively fashioned from bamboo. Tina poured herself a cup of tea and added cream from a little silver pitcher. She smiled at Topaz. 'You're Joe's wife, aren't you?' she said.

'Yes, ma'am, that I am.' Topaz rolled her eyes, back-slanting and moistly dark. 'He's like a big kid most times, but all right, I guess.'

Tina laughed and sipped her tea, which was a trifle weak and brewed she suspected from tea-bags. 'I thought he seemed very nice, and very able. Have you both worked here at Blue Water House a long time?'

'I got dis job only since you come, missus,' Topaz ran proud, pink-palmed hands down the crisp sides of her blue and white uniform. 'I'm a housemaid a long time. Joe, he done mos' jobs roun' about

Blue Water since Mr. John come take over. Joe, he's very attached to dis place and de folks—' Then Topaz seemed to realize that as a personal maid she had to be a little more dignified and less chatty, and Tina watched with a grin as the coloured woman rustled importantly to the tallboy and took fresh underthings out of one of the sandalwood drawers. The possession of a personal maid went with her position here, Tina supposed, and she wondered if John had given the job to Topaz because in her inexperience she wouldn't be likely to make Tina uncomfortable.

It would be like him to be thoughtful in that respect, for the servants here would be quick to realize that his second wife was quite unused to life in a big house. That being waited on was something that made her feel shy and confused.

'Most of my things were left on the motor-launch last night, Topaz,' she said, 'so I shall have to wear my suit again.'

Topaz put out the coral jacket and skirt in readiness, then as she drew a bath for Tina she forgot her dignity and hummed one of the island calypsos. Her spry cheerfulness, combined with the bright sunshine, helped roll away last night's clouds for Tina, soon splashing in the step-down tub of the bathroom she was to share with John. It was tiled in black and white, with a shower cabinet, a deep towelling chair, and a glass-topped toilet table holding various toiletries.

As Tina squeezed water over her shoulders with a big sponge she reflected that she had at least the small kicks of being in love. There was John's shaving-tackle and hairwash beside her fat jar of moisturizing cream. His bathrobe slung on a hook with hers, a shirt button on the floor near the linen basket.

She soaped a slim leg and wriggled her toes. She was Tina Trecarrel, and all this was actually real! Some minutes later she was stepping out of the tub as knuckles rapped the door.

'Ahoy there!' It was John. 'Joe and I have just brought up your baggage.'

'Oh, lovely!' The mirror above the toilet table reflected Tina's startled, mermaid-wet nudity and blazing cheeks. 'Start breakfast if you're famished, John. I'll dry off and be right out.'

She thought he might be leaning with a shoulder to the door, for she heard his answering laugh quite clearly. 'A woman's "right out" is like the islanders' "now-now"—meaning in half an hour. I've had breakfast laid on the balcony of the lounge. Did you sleep well?'

'Splendidly, thank you.' She was now towelling herself and thankfully reflecting that he sounded in a good mood.

'I'll go and see if the kiddie's awake. She might enjoy breakfasting with us. Okay?'

'Oh, yes. I was going to suggest that to you, John.'

'Were you?' His laughter was faintly sardonic. Then there was silence and Tina knew he had gone out of her bedroom. She talcumed off, then went in to dress. Topaz was busily unpacking her suitcases and she chuckled away to herself as she stood one of Tina's shoes on the palm of her hand.

'You have the smallest foot I ever see, ma'am. You jus' take a look at that, now.'

Tina slipped into the pastel dress Topaz had laid out in place of her suit and zipped the waist. 'I'm afraid there isn't much of me,' she agreed. 'Toss over those beige sandals, please.'

Topaz, however, was determined to take her duties seriously and she insisted on helping Tina into the sandals, a comfortable beach pair from her Chorley days, for John and Liza might go exploring with her.

'You like me to fix your gold hair, ma'am?' Topaz coaxed, and Tina submitted after warning her maid not to take too long. The large, pink-palmed hands were curiously soothing and gentle, and Tina asked Topaz if she had any children.

'Coupla kids. They're at school, ma'am.' Topaz beamed at her young mistress's reflection in the mirror as she swirled the bamboo-straight hair to the crown of her head and fixed it with a ribbon. 'You find that more refreshin'—why, you don' look more'n a kid yourself, Mis' Trecarrel.' Then a rather shy expression crept into the dark brown eyes. 'We were all wonderin' what you be like—wait I tell Aspasia.'

'Who's Aspasia?'

'She's my friend down in the village, ma'am. She work here when Mis' Joanna alive. She care personal for Mis' Joanna.'

Tina went still as a bird, then edging her tongue round lips that had gone rather dry, she said: 'Was this room very different when the first Mrs. Trecarrel had it?'

'Dis room, ma'am?' Topaz shot Tina a look of surprise as she tidied the dressing table. 'Why, bless you, dis ain't Mis' Joanna's room. She slep' on the other side of Blue Water, where de sea sound reach her. She love de sea—maybe too much!'

Tina shivered at these words, with the undertone of dark meaning Topaz superstitiously gave them. 'What was she like?' The words escaped from Tina before she could stop them. 'I mean—was she kind?'

'I reckon Mis' Joanna okay to work for.' Topaz arranged Tina's brush and comb with exactitude on the lace mat. 'She have long hair lak' dark red silk, an' Aspasia say she brush an' brush it until it near sparkled. She lak' Miss Paula to look at, only more beautiful.' Topaz shook a regretful head and pressed a hand to her scooped cheek. 'I recall de way dem peacocks cryin' de night before Mis' Joanna done get drowned. Dem peacocks cryin' lak' dat a sure sign there goin' to be trouble. I tell Joe, and dat why he near when dat big barracuda snap at Mr. John's leg. Joe he kill dat tiger fish. Why, we think Mr. John goin' to die as well, him laid real low from loss of blood an' shock . . .'

Tina went cold, for her maid's sing-song

English painted a scene so vivid that she felt she had been on the shore that morning to witness John's struggle to save Joanna. She saw him cutting through the blue silk of water that creamed, red-tinged, when a silver-grey streak flashed up from among the roots of the coral and took his left leg in tooth-filled jaws. Had John cried out Joanna's name ... in love and despair ... or guilt?

She found herself in the adjoining room and walked to the open glass doors of the balcony. John and his daughter had finished breakfast, and with an elbow propped on the circular table he was talking about his trip to England. Liza, her gaze fixed lovingly upon his face, was taking nibbles at a creamy custard-apple while she listened to him.

Tina paused to watch them for a moment, their dark heads close together, the child in pirate pants and a sundust halter-top, John looking lean and hard in beige slacks and a short-sleeve tan silk shirt. The deep warmth of his voice carried to Tina, while his hair was rough from his swim. Love was so certain in her that whatever he had said last night had to be forgotten. Not to forget was to hand Paula a minor victory.

Then John glanced up and took in rapidly the fresh picture Tina presented in her apricot dress with its scooped neck and cutaway sleeves, his rings winking so new on the hand she held against her. He rose to his feet and held in readiness one of the cushioned, wrought-iron chairs. 'You look very nice,' he said. 'Doesn't she, Liza?'

Tina knew he was just being polite, for as she stepped on to the balcony and was dappled by the sunlight the gleam that stole into her husband's sea-blue eyes was an indulgent one. Her delight was mixed, but intense, and she had to look away from him—flinching almost from her own inward storm of emotion. 'Good morning, Liza!' She gave her smile and her attention to the child.

'Good morning, Tina.' A shy smile touched Liza's face to a charm that held a latent beauty. 'Is it all right for me to call you—just that? One of my friends at school has a stepmother and she has to call her *Auntie*.'

Tina slipped into her seat at the table, murmuring thank you to John, her fair head bent as she removed her napkin from its ivory ring. 'I don't feel in the least like your auntie, Liza.' She exchanged a quick smile with the child. 'More like a big sister—mmm, I think I'll try some bacon and a ring or two of pineapple.'

As she helped herself from the covered dish she was conscious of Liza's interested scrutiny, then a thin, tanned arm came edging near hers and Liza gave a chuckle. 'How pale you look compared to Pops and me,' she exclaimed.

'I intend to get just as brown as you two, you just wait. Your bracelet looks pretty, Liza,' Tina added. 'Have you unpacked your other presents yet?'

'I've peeked at my saddle. It's a beauty, isn't it? Sorrel will fancy himself when I put it on his back.' Liza hugged her knees and treated her father to a mischievous grin. 'You did do a lot of shopping in England, Pops. I must say I like the present you brought back for yourself.'

'The youngsters these days!' he muttered behind a laugh, catching Tina's eye. 'There my dear, you have the approval you were so worried about. Yes, Liza, Tina was naturally worried in case you chose not to like her.'

'That's funny,' Liza touched a finger to Tina's ruby ring, 'I thought she might be snooty and not care for someone else's child. Isn't it a relief, Tina, that you're so super?'

'Am I?' Tina's smile was warm but startled.

'You bet!' Liza rocked herself in her young eagerness. 'You aren't all painted up a-and pretentious. I'd have had it in for Pops if he'd married someone like that.'

There was such a fierce, meaning note in the child's voice that Tina had to look at John to see if he realized what lay behind her outburst. His gaze was fixed upon Liza, so intent and searching that a quick chill feathered through Tina. Yes, he knew his daughter disliked Paula Carrish. That could be part of the reason why he fought his own desires in that direction—why he had given her a young, uncomplicated stepmother!

Then, thrusting a hand into a back pocket of his trousers, he drew out his tobacco pouch. 'D'you mind if I enjoy a pipe while you're eating, Tina?' he asked.

She shook her head. Her appetite had slackened off, anyway, and she had to force down the last crisp portion of bacon. Like a dark shadow, Paula Carrish seemed to hover above every sunbeam that came out for her! She topped up her coffee cup and asked Liza how long a holiday she had.

'Two weeks. Super, isn't it? The three of us will be able to have crowds of fun.'

'We'll have to teach Tina how to ride,' John said, biting on the nickel stem of his briar and carrying a match to the bowl. 'That little filly, Dusky, should be okay for her to start on, wouldn't you say, pet?'

Liza bobbed her head. 'Didn't you learn how to ride back in England, Tina?'

'I'm afraid not.' Tina smiled and dabbed at her lips with her napkin. 'There are a lot of things I–I haven't yet coped with, so you'll both have to be patient with me.' She shot a look at John, but he rose in that moment and went to the balcony parapet . . . as though moved to irritation by her shy appeal. Heat ran over her body. You could hate love, she fiercely reflected. It ruthlessly destroyed your self-dependence and left you as exposed to every small thrust as a crab without its shell!

Then John swung round and puffed out smoke, the brilliant sunshine behind him, his eyes in the dense shadow of his brows. 'What do you fancy doing this morning, Tina?' he asked.

'I'd rather like to do a tour of the house

and get the feel of things,' she replied.

'Good idea.' He spoke rather carelessly. 'Liza can be your guide. I have some mail to catch up with, but this afternoon we'll go for a drive round the island—'

'And have tea at Smuggler's Cove?' Liza entreated. 'They serve super cream ices.'

'Don't you ever get tired of stuffing yourself?' He quirked an eyebrow at his daughter, who was peeling a banana with the tip of her tongue showing between her red lips. He tweaked her hair on his way into the house, then paused to add: 'If the pair of you go down for a swim, be sure to keep within the barrier reef. Joe's seen a couple of small sharks lurking about just lately. They probably won't come inside the reef, the fishing isn't good enough, but they might still be on the prowl beyond it. Also Tina will need to be well daubed with sun oil. Take some with you and be sure she smarms plenty on the vulnerable spots, like the backs of her knees and that bit of a nose.'

Tina felt her heart quickening at the deepening pitch to his voice, but when she braved a meeting with his eyes there was a merciless amusement in them. She jerked back when he flicked a light finger at her nose. 'Don't treat me like the baby around here, John,' she protested.

'I'm only warning you that your nose will peel if you don't oil it.' He looked mock innocent. 'See you later, my infants.'

He strolled into the house, leaving behind him a trail of tobacco smoke and a giggling daughter. 'Isn't Pops funny?' she said through a mouthful of banana.

'Madly comic!' Tina, pink-cheeked, rolled her napkin and inserted it in its ring, nerves of annoyance and frustration rippling through her. Back in England he had said he wanted a wife, not a little girl to dandle on his knee, yet now she was here with him he was treating her as though he was no longer certain what he wanted of her. A most unsatisfactory state of affairs.

A houseboy in crisp white came to clear the breakfast table, and Tina went with Liza on a tour of her new home. Last night she had absorbed only a surface impression of its grace and charm, now in daylight she discovered that it was mellow-stoned, embraced by a spacious suntrap of a veranda, with an impressive pillared portico. Liza made eager dashes from room to room, catching at Tina's hand and pointing out things—the chairs in the hall with little medieval paintings set in the backs of them, the steep bookcase windows in the library, and the side table supported on a carved eagle. The jewelled chandeliers and Queen Anne love-seats in the drawing-room. The lovely rose windows at the curves of the double staircase, framing at one side a sweeping view of Blue Water's grounds; at the other side a spectacular gold, white and blue mosaic that was the sugar-icing beach and ruffled silk ocean below the house.

'This is my den,' Liza announced, throwing open the door of a charming mimosa room with a pair of scarlet basket-chairs, curly white rugs beside the divan bed, a sprig-skirted dressing table with a stool to match, and a balding teddy-bear beside a blonde doll on the padded window-seat. The room of a much-loved child, Tina thought, noticing the carved toys and musical boxes John had brought back for Liza from Continental trips.

'Make yourself at home and I'll play you a record,' Liza said, patting one of her basket-chairs, then sliding open a well-stocked record cabinet.

Tina smilingly listened while Liza enthused about her various pop idols, already loving this child who was part of John. So much a part of him, with the same promise of long, easy limbs, a wide sensitive beauty about the mouth, blue eyes contrasting with dense lashes.

'Do you know what an iconoclast is?' Liza suddenly asked, squatting on a plump floor cushion like a gnome and gazing up at Tina.

'Isn't it a breaker of images?' Tina smiled. 'Have you been learning about them at school?'

'I saw it in a book,' Liza gestured towards her bookcase. 'Paula's like that, isn't she?'

The statement shook Tina. 'Why do you say that, Liza?' she asked, shot through with a quick fear in case the woman had said something to the child about her father.

Liza shrugged her thin shoulders. 'When people are happy she sort of pulls them down. She does it with Uncle Ralph, and he's a darling. I wish he'd get married, then she'd have to move out of his bungalow.' Liza caught at Tina's left hand and pressed her cheek to it. 'I used to be scared Pops would marry her. Ooh, I bet she's all steamed up because he hasn't.'

Tina cupped the young, warm cheek and reflected that children, like animals, had infallible instincts when it came to judging people. It was almost as though they could smell insincerity and cruelty, and there wasn't much doubt in Tina's mind that there was a streak of cruelty in Paula Carrish. She thought of the woman in her leopard cape last night, elegant and extraordinary, standing before John on her long silken legs and looking him straight in the eye. What had she been daring him to remember? Tina dragged her mind away from the scene.

'Shall we go down on the beach?' she suggested. 'I want to start getting a tan.'

'Yes, let's.' Liza jumped to her feet. 'And we mustn't forget the sun oil, otherwise, being so fair, you'll be bound to burn.'

Tina went along to her room to change into her swimwear, a ruched pink one-piece, over which she threw a towelling poncho. She also took along her smoked glasses, but didn't bother about a cap, for she liked to feel the sea in her hair when she swam. Having lived near the sea all her life she had learned to swim as a child and was very able in the water.

They made their way through the garden to the cliff steps, and Tina saw her first flame trees, burning with bold beauty against the hot blue sky. There were silver wattles, and gloriously scented magnolias. And a really striking-looking tree called shower of gold, with cascades of sunny buds and glossy green leaves. Big butterflies clung to the peachy frangipani and cool blue plumbago, while the incessant tuck-tuck of a hidden Blue-Hood followed them.

'Everything is so vivid,' Tina exclaimed in wonder. 'Flowers never grow to this size in England. And the scents! They make me feel drunk.'

'Did you mind leaving England?' Liza asked.

'I wanted to come to St. Monique from the first moment your father described the island to me,' Tina replied. 'It was a chilly day in March, and I never dreamed at that time that he would marry me and actually bring me here.'

'It's like a fairy tale,' Liza cried, running across the warm feathery sand with Tina behind her. They chased into the blue and buoyant water and swam to the lacing of foam about the barrier reef, where the coral was as jewelled as the tails of the peacocks Tina had watched with John in Holland Park Gardens. They had been happy together that day, his fingers catching at hers as though, like a lover, he needed the reassurance of touching her.

Back on the beach, after feasting their eyes on the colourful fish that haunted the reef, Tina and the child dried off, oiled each other and stretched out in the sun. The sand was soft as lambswool under Tina's body, and for now she was lazy with contentment as she lay listening to the breakers rolling silver over the coral reef.

* * *

After lunch up at the house, John had the car driven round to the front steps. The car he had used in England had been a hired one, and Tina's eyes widened at the dashing open-top vehicle waiting below the double tier of steps leading down from the portico. It was glossily cream, upholstered in saxe-blue, with a silver Mercury on the bonnet.

There was room for the three of them on the wide front seat, and as John slid in behind the wheel and slammed the door he cast a side-glance over his passengers. Tina wore cream glazed cotton, Liza peppermint-green, and wide Alice bands held their hair in place. Both of them sat waiting like small demure girls for their treat to begin.

'Do we look nice, Pops?' Liza inquired.

'Like a pair of vanilla and peppermint lollies,' he grinned. 'Mighty eatable!'

He started the car and they swept round a small plantation of tropical plants in the centre of the drive and out on to a highway of crushed coral. The countryside through which they drove was fertile with plantations of sweet potatoes, sugar cane, maize and bananas. The sails of the maize mills turned lazily in the warm air, and narrow village streets set with gingerbread houses were wrapped in the somnolence of siesta. Dogs stirred in the heat, grubbing their muzzles into fleabitten coats, while a coloured farm boy quizzed the touring car from beneath the ragged brim of a straw hat, then lolled back against a lime-washed wall and resumed his doze.

'D'you see the way he looked at us?' John smiled. 'He knows it's true about mad dogs and Englishmen, but I've never succumbed to the island habit of resting while the sun's at its zenith. Feeling the heat yet, Tina?'

'I love it!' she replied warmly. 'England starves one of sunshine.'

She saw small farm holdings clinging to the hillsides, tumble-down but picturesque; peaceful yet with a hint of the pagan about them. They drove along a headland that plunged to the turbulent surf of a coast where wrecking had gone on in the bad old days, and John said: 'This part of the island reminds me of Cornwall. Even its history of wrecking and pirates is much the same.'

He stopped the car because Liza wanted to pick wild flowers—as though they didn't have enough in their own garden—and strolled long-legged with Tina towards a grassy patch that gave a spectacular view of the ocean and was green enough to promise a breeze while they rested there. John sprawled, indolent and easy-limbed, white shirt open at his throat. Tina sat with her legs neatly curled in front of her, fingers plucking at the grass, her gaze on the sea rippling round the glossy points of rock—to which ships had been lured in the old days by the lanterns of wreckers. The mewing calls of the swooping birds and the sobbing sea were like echoes down the years of the people who clung, drowning, to bits and pieces of floating timber.

John suddenly touched her hand and said softly: 'Look at Liza.'

Tina did so. The child had plucked a flower that evidently pleased her very much, and quite unconscious of being observed she was stroking its soft petals against her cheek with the youthful wonderment that is all too soon lost in the stresses of adult living.

'How I'd love to sculpt the child just as she is now,' John murmured. 'But that kind of pose could never be recaptured. See, already she's moving on to her next discovery.'

'Couldn't you work from memory?' Tina asked gently.

'Memory is too—too fallible.' He shrugged his shoulders, drew up his knees and encircled them with his arms. 'You capture some facets, but others are lost in an inevitable obscurity and you have a piece of art which is flawed instead of perfect. Art only truly succeeds when it satisfies the heart, the mind, and the soul. It's a kind of loving, and a creator of art, like a maker of love, must be without doubts, otherwise there can't be true satisfaction for creator or lover.'

Tina's heart jolted. She had caught the deepening note of meaning in John's voice and was sure he was telling her that until doubts were cleared away between them, they could not be close... That was the decision he had come to, and she, in her shyness, her inexperience, her pain, had to abide by it. She had her pride as well.

Assuming self-possession like a garment, she launched into a question that had cropped up in her mind that morning. 'Will it be all right if I do my own marketing?' she asked. 'It would be rather nice for you and Liza to have English cooking now and again, and I'd enjoy doing it. Topaz could go with me to the shops.'

'Sure you can do your own marketing!' He ran lazily amused eyes over her slightly tense face. 'You don't have to get my permission to make changes in your own home—I'm not a Victorian tyrant like that aunt of yours.'

'I know *that*.' She gave one of his elkthong sandals a light kick. 'But I'm a comparative stranger on the scene, and men get into routines they don't always like having disturbed.'

'It shouldn't disrupt me too much having steak and kidney pie now and again. The cook hasn't a light hand with pastry, and I'm partial. I like jam-puff as well, now we're on the subject.' He stretched out and gave her chin a tweak. 'Reassured, my timid one?'

She nodded, but was prompted to add: 'All the same, you know, you men can be unnerving creatures at times.'

His eyebrows shot up, then on a half-laugh he said: 'If I unnerve you a little, it's only because I'm older and experienced, but I haven't forgotten your telling me you hadn't much to do with men owing to your aunt's dislike of the sex.' His mouth grew mocking. 'If you can't cotton to the various hints I've thrown out about keeping my distance for a while, then you can always shoot the bolt on your bedroom door. I doubt whether I could batter down solid teak.'

'There's no need to say things like that.' Colour ran hotly to her temples. 'I assure you I've taken your hints.'

'Then we can drop the subject.' A hint of steel edged the words, and Tina sighed with relief when Liza appeared on the scene, her collection of flowers and weeds raining into Tina's lap.

'Whew, I'm hot!' she announced.

'Then settle down and cool off,' John ordered.

Liza squatted and cast a glance from her father to Tina. Her eyebrows disappeared into her fringe. 'Don't tell me you two have been having a tiff already?' she demanded.

'Of course we haven't.' Tina avoided John's eye and fiddled with the flowers in her lap. 'Shall I make you a coronet of these little blue flowers, Liza?' she asked.

And while John lay back on the grass, his arms pillowed under his head, Tina wove the flowers into a circlet watched by Liza. A little later they drove to the seashore restaurant called Smuggler's Cove and sitting at a table under a giant rainbow sunshade they had long cool drinks and cream ices. Tina tried to feel relaxed, but she succeeded only with an effort.

The sky was like rose-tinged silk when they returned to the car and big sea-birds hovered above the sheet of gold that was the sea. Far off the mountains of Jamaica were a purple chain. A glorious scene, lost too quickly in the twilight that comes so suddenly to hot climates. On the way home, Liza's sleepy head rested against

Tina, and the weight and warmth of the child was food for Tina's hungering spirit. She encircled her with an arm, but John at the wheel remained aloof from what she had to offer. And because she was young, sensitive, and afraid of intruding, she left him to his thoughts and they drove on through the star-dusted, palm-fringed dusk in silence.

*   *   *

Marketing with Topaz turned out to be a thoroughly diverting and interesting experience. They were chauffeured as far as the wharf by one of John's servants, where Tina told him to wait, then she and Topaz made their way along the crowded quay where the air was salty from the glistening loads of snapper and kingfish being swung out of the holds of the fishing boats, and lively with the work chants of the strapping, coloured seamen.

Topaz loped along beside Tina, a head-basket balanced on a plaited fibre-ring, her strawberry-pink shirtwaister blending with the smooth coffee of her throat and arms. Tina wore a shady hat, but already she was moist from the heat and felt her dress clinging between her shoulder-blades. Maybe she was crazy to take on this task, but there were too many indications that she could develop into a nonentity around Blue Water House unless she exerted herself. The butler and the cook had turned sour at first, when she had interviewed them in the kitchen quarters that morning, but she had stuck to her guns. She was the missus, but if she allowed them to overrule her, they would do so with impunity.

'Mr. John complain about de food I make?' the cook had demanded aggressively, looking on the verge of snatching off his white cap and apron.

'You're a good cook, Jason,' Tina had soothed him, 'but I want to show you some English cooking. I'm sure yams, marrows and sweet potatoes can be baked and stuffed, but I've been told that you dish them up boiled all the time.'

The cook's eyes had looked rather boiled at that remark. 'Dey fine like dat,' he had exploded.

'Certainly, a couple of times a week,' she agreed. 'I'm not trying to put your back up, Jason, but I'm sure you have Mr. John's interest at heart almost as much as I have, and it will be nice to give him a wider variety of meals.'

And because the West Indian temperament, the male one, is hot on wives pandering to husbands, Jason suddenly showed a part of the wide smile he was capable of and allowed her to inspect the store cupboard and its contents. She had discovered a singular lack of preserves and jams. On such an island, where the fruit was so luscious but where unfortunately it so easily spoiled, she considered it a great waste not to preserve some of it for pies and flans. She had told Topaz that she wished to order a batch of fruit, and they were making their way to the store the coloured woman considered the most reliable. Topaz was shrewd and Tina was content to rely on her judgment.

They arrived at the square where the stores and stallholders were congregated. The atmosphere was noisy and haggling; brash and spicy with a mixture of aromas, the colourful native wares and foods meeting the eye at every turn. Pork, salt fish-cakes, the orange meat of sea-eggs, corn and cassava. The kind of food Tina suspected John had been living on, eating to satisfy his hunger, poor darling, and vaguely craving the steak and kidney pie he had said he was partial to. Spotting a grocery store with a butchery section, Tina decided then and there to buy steak and the rest of the ingredients for a thoroughly English dinner that evening.

Back in England, Tina's aunt had done most of the shopping, and this morning she experienced her first wifely delight of having a plump purse with which to slash out on a jar of brandied peaches, a huge coral and cream lobster, a tin of asparagus, a deep yellow and scarlet Dutch cheese, some dark, delicious-looking gherkins .. into the large basket carried by Topaz went a variety of eatables with which to woo her husband, while a tiny smile clung to the corners of her mouth. Over at the butchery section she thought it wise to let the more experienced Topaz select the chuck steak and kidneys, then she decided that a chicken would be nice for tomorrow evening. Topaz prodded the breastbone of the bird the butcher was extolling and, finding it hard, loudly demanded to be shown another. 'We want tender meat, not ole crow,' she informed him spiritedly.

On the way back to the car, with Topaz carrying the shopping on her head, Tina wondered if Joanna had done her own marketing. Somehow she couldn't imagine it. Instinctively she knew that in every way she was different from the woman who had hair like dark red silk, who had loved the sea in all its moods, who had been at home in the saddle, at the tiller of a boat, at the foot of a table of guests at Blue Water House. A gracious hostess, a vivacious wife, a popular friend. She had surely been all three—yet something had gone wrong between her and John.

Tina screwed her handkerchief in a moist hand and felt certain Paula Carrish had caused that rift. From what Ralph Carrish had said it was evident that Joanna had been highly strung and easily aroused to distrust, and Paula had often posed for John in the privacy of his studio. No ordinary woman, but one whose female magnetism reached out like a caress when she looked at a man. What more easy than for her to insinuate poison into Joanna's suggestible mind?

'Dahling ... fancy seeing you!' That seductive voice with the dropped r's was unmistakable, and Tina knew she lost colour as long fingers were laid on her arm and she met a pair of green eyes beneath the wide brim of a crystal straw hat. Paula! A patronizing smile on her thin ruby lips, and clad in cool jade-green shantung with jade stones swinging in her ear-lobes.

'Hullo, Miss Carrish.' Tina had to force herself to sound amiable. 'As you can see, I've been doing some marketing.'

'Heavens, how conscientious of you—on your honeymoon!' Paula flickered a smile over Tina's face, with little tendrils of pale hair clinging to her hot, damp forehead. 'I always do my marketing by phone, but you new little brides are always bursting to please with a fledgling eagerness, aren't you? What a shame the gilt's already off the gingerbread for John!' Paula's fingers tightened meaningly on the fine bones of Tina's wrist. 'I shouldn't waste the energy, my dear. Keeping young in a sub-tropical climate means keeping cool, and right now you look in need of a long iced booster. I'm on my way to the Spindrift Club for a cocktail, so how about joining me? We should get to know each other—' The woman gave a throaty little laugh. 'After all, I'm one of your husband's *closest* friends.'

The meaning behind those words wasn't lost on Tina. She was meant to accept them as a challenge, and she did so. 'A long cool drink would be welcome, Miss Carrish,' she replied, squarely meeting the green eyes that glimmered beneath languorous, tinted lids.

'The name is Paula, my dear.' The long fingers slipped away from Tina's wrist. 'You and I must not be formal—I'm sure we're going to find we have several things in common.'

Tina shivered, and camouflaged it by turning quickly to her maid, who had fallen back a few paces. The dark eyes of the coloured woman were fixed upon Paula, and Tina surprised a look of antagonism in them before Topaz assumed a polite, listening look as Tina told her to go along home in the car. 'Tell my husband where I am if he asks, Topaz,' she added. 'Say I'll pick up a cab.'

'Yes, ma'am.' Topaz then loped off along the wharf, swinging her arms and seemingly unaware of the heavy basket of goods on her crinkly head.

'Primitive creatures, aren't they?' Paula drawled.

Not only they, Tina thought, falling into step beside the tall, lance-thin figure who had the faintly undulating walk and hardly discernible bosom of the models Tina had watched with Gaye Lanning when they had gone shopping for her trousseau. All that seemed to have happened in another life—Chorley—the empty years with Aunt Maud. Only the here and now was real. The glitter of the sun on the tourmaline clasp of Paula's bag. Her shadowed profile under the wide brim of her hat, pale as white jade except for the ruby slash of a mouth . . .

There was hate in her, Tina felt. The kind that has its birth from the pangs of a frustrated love. It was eating at her heart like a canker . . . it made her a dangerous woman with the weapon of some secret knowledge aimed at Tina's vulnerable heart.

CHAPTER SIX

PAULA was a member of the Spindrift Club, and on their way through the long modern cocktail lounge she was hailed by various acquaintances who treated Tina to long stares of frank curiosity. Paula introduced her to a planter and his wife, neighbours she obviously didn't wish to offend, but she seemed eager to talk to Tina alone and made charming excuses not to linger when the couple invited them to have a drink.

They finally settled into wicker chairs out on the canopied observation deck, which overlooked the private beach that shelved to the sea where bronzed young people were skimming the surf on narrow boards. 'Join me in a Sangaree,' Paula suggested when a waiter came to take their order. 'It's a drink I recommend.'

Tina nodded, unaware that wine and curaçao were mixed in the concoction which eventually arrived in highball glasses tinkling with ice and decorated with lime slices and nutmeg. Tina chewed a pretzel and gazed down, unrelaxed, at the sun-baskers and surfers. One sun-tanned giant was riding the glistening curves of aquamarine with a superb nonchalance, his lionesque blond head thrown back, his wide-shouldered, lean-hipped body somehow pagan in its lithe grace as he shot over the glassy corrugations.

Paula was also watching him as she fitted a cigarette into a jade holder and flicked a matching lighter at the tip. 'Impressive male animal, isn't he?' she drawled. 'Men like that usually haven't a thought in their heads beyond fun and females, but Dacier d'Andremont is an interesting exception. There's very good blood in him, I believe, and the d'Andremont property on Martinique is said to be extensive.'

'It's unusual for a Frenchman to have such light-coloured hair, isn't it?' Tina remarked, taking a sip at her drink and blinking a little at its potency.

'He's an unusual guy in several respects,' Paula tapped ash from her cigarette with a fingernail enamelled to match the jade holder. 'Despite all that physical attraction, he's the invulnerable type who can take women or leave them, and most women find such a man a perpetual challenge. Each one feels he should settle for matrimony—with her. Talking about matrimony, how are you settling down as a wife?'

Here it came, Tina thought, the probing into John's second marriage. Paula could no more keep away from it than the golden bees that zoomed into the trumpets of flowers cloaking a wall near Tina.

'Quite well,' she said brightly. 'I'm firm friends with Liza already.'

'And with John, of course?' Paula insinuated softly.

The question was a double-edged probe, and Tina met it with the pluck of desperation. 'Naturally we're friends,' she replied. 'Don't you think husbands and wives should be?'

'Only with other husbands and wives, my dear.' Paula had slipped from indolence into alertness without moving a muscle of her graceful body, but it was evident in the emerald glint of her eyes and the way the tip of her cigarette went danger red. 'Being pals is all right in a placid set-up, but hardly possible in a passionate one. A girl might as well stay with her mother if that's the kind of relationship she wants with a man.'

'My mother's dead,' Tina said, aware that all she could do was fight edged wit with blunt honesty. 'I was brought up by an aunt, and I assure you I prefer being with John.'

'You've always worked for your living, eh?' Paula swung a long, slim foot in a black patent shoe, flicked away ash with a fingernail that had never broken on the keyboard of a typewriter, exuded a perfume that had probably cost several pounds for a couple of ounces. 'Were you a shopgirl—something like that?'

Tina's skin prickled with antagonism at the way Paula looked and spoke, while her fingers tightened on her drink until her nails slowly drained of their natural coral-pink. 'I was a shorthand-typist, Miss Carrish,' she replied stiffly, wishing she dared tag on that even had she been fortunate enough to possess a brother in a well-paid position she would never have made a hanger-on of herself and then presumed to act the lady bountiful with other people.

'A typist, eh?' The narrowed green eyes raked Tina and found nothing in her that might appeal to a man; obviously all she saw was the self-consciousness, the angularity of lingering adolescence, the retreating look of a kitten who had learned long ago to keep mischief and love to herself. 'You've landed quite a large fish for small bait, haven't you, my dear?' Cigarette smoke slipped from the thin blaze of a mouth, hanging on the air with that deliberate remark.

Tina heard the words and felt witless, impotently aware that when she was no longer face to face with this woman she would find herself manufacturing quite a few barbed answers. 'I-I didn't marry John because I was after a meal ticket, if that's what you're implying,' she fought back. 'It wouldn't matter to me if he wasn't a clever sculptor a-and quite well off.'

'Oh, don't kid me you don't like your cake nice and plummy!' Ice tinkled . . . the ice in Paula's drink mixing with the chips in her voice. 'John almost didn't take that trip to England . . . he suffers quite a bit with his left leg, but then, of course, you must know that.'

Ice trickled down Tina's spine—she hadn't known it!

'I guess you happened along,' Paula drawled, 'just as John was noticing a few threads of silver in his hair and needing the reassurance of men of his age—that he's still able to attract a chick. It's a love affair with most men. You're to be congratulated on hooking him legally.'

'Thank you.' Tina spoke without conscious irony, her thoughts with John, who told her so little about what pleased and hurt him. Paula knew so much more about him than she did, and the knowledge left a bitter taste her drink could not dispel. A pulse hammered in her temple and she took off her hat and shook back her hair, wanting through it the breeze that was stirring the fronded, sinuous palms down on the beach. The blond giant in white trunks no longer formed part of the sapphire and silver mosaic . . .

'Why don't you have your hair cut and styled?' Paula remarked. 'Long hair without a natural wave is inclined to look rather lank.'

Her own sienna tresses were coiled into a rich knot at the nape of her neck, and Tina, tired of being needled, got back with a jab. 'John has specially asked me not to have my hair cut,' she replied. 'He likes it this way.'

'But it makes you look like an illustration for Alice in Wonderland!' Paula laughed glossily. 'John didn't marry you just to give Liza a sister, did he?'

'I certainly hope so!' Tina's usually quiet temper was having an edge put on it, and she managed to inject into those four words a meaning Paula couldn't fail to understand. She saw the shock of her implication drill through the other woman, who sat very still, gazing fixedly at the ocean, then the picture changed as swiftly as it does on a screen and her long white hand was signalling the waiter to bring repeats of the potent Sangaree. Tina wanted to refuse a second drink, to rise and run, frantic as a mouse that had dared to pop out of its hole. Her fingernails dug into the straw brim of her hat.

'I'd rather like to show you something.' Paula flicked open her bag and took out a small case that opened to show a pair of coloured photographs set side by side. She handed the case to Tina, who took it with a hand that showed the state of her nerves. The man was unmistakably John... When he had been the husband of the girl in the frame beside him.

Tina was lost to her surroundings as she gazed at the photograph, absorbing every detail of the fascinating face. The wing-shaped eyebrows, enormous hazelgreen eyes, small chiselled nose and rich red curve of a mouth. And the hair! Glossy, sienna-brown like Paula's, but softly clouding about the slim white throat. Tina's heart was painfully squeezed, for Joanna had been lovely and appealing, a man's dream of heaven on earth!

'My cousin,' Paula said. 'John's first wife—who was drowned.'

'I know.' Tina's throat ached with pain. 'She was beautiful. John once told me she was, but there's a certain coldness about the word, one thinks of chiselled perfection alone—but how warm, how alive, how vivid she looks.'

Paula was holding the fresh drink the waiter had placed in front of her, suspended midway between the raffia coaster and her mouth. 'Has John talked much about Joanna?' she asked sharply.

Still a trifle dazed, Tina glanced up. She shook her head. Joanna's death had not only been the destruction of a beautiful person, but there had been a rift John had wanted to cross, back into happiness with his wife, and fate had irrevocably widened it. The pain of that was always with him—it overshadowed Tina's marriage.

She clicked shut the little case holding the photographs and handed it back to Paula. The emerald fingernails glinted against the silver, then it was out of sight in her purse, but not out of mind. That was why she had showed it, Tina supposed. To let her see what she was up against . . . or more likely as a warning that she, Paula, was capable of enticing a man away from a lovely woman, let alone a plain one!

It was at this point that deep, gay, attractively accented tones dropped into the silence that had fallen between Tina and Paula. 'May I join you ladies?' said the voice.

Tina glanced up, startled, straight into a pair of yellow-brown eyes under a cropped thatch of raw-gold hair. Immaculate cream drill sat on shoulders so broad they made Tina blink, while a quick white smile cut clefts in the hard, tanned face. Decidedly not a man who was instantly forgettable, and every bit as spectacular as he had looked skimming the aquamarine waves in his swimming trunks.

'Dacier!' Paula smiled and held out a slim hand, which he took and carried to his lips. 'You may certainly join us. What are you drinking?'

'I have told the waiter to bring me a Rhum Clément,' he smiled down, letting go of her hand with attractive reluctance.

'You were that sure we would want you, eh?' Paula drawled.

'A man who is sure is always acceptable to women.' The audacity of his grin swept from Paula to Tina. 'Will you not introduce me to this delightful child?'

Tina's ringed left hand was in her lap, her skin was shiny, her hair pushed carelessly behind her ears. Very likely she did look a child to this sophisticate with the boyishly wicked, pale-sherry eyes. His

French blood made him tag on a compliment.

'This is John Trecarrel's bride,' Paula informed him. 'Tina, meet Dacier d'Andremont, that dangerous bachelor I was telling you about.'

'How do you do, Mr. d'Andremont?' Tina tried hard not to give in to her infuriating habit of blushing, but he was the type of man who could have made even Paula blush, had he wished. Her right hand received the warm touch of his lips, then he parked himself beside her and gave her a long, frank scrutiny. 'So you are the bride about whom everyone on St. Monique has been speculating? I am charmed to know you, Mrs. Trecarrel.'

'Thank you.' Tina gave him her shy but direct smile and was willing to bet that he had singed dozens of wings in his thirty-odd years without once getting within entanglement distance of the matrimonial net. A charmer, a dangerous one, if you weren't already on love's hook as firmly as she was.

His drink was brought to the table and as he raised his glass to Tina, he said: 'There is an old Andalusian saying about marriage which has always amused me, that they are like melons and in every hundred you will find a good one. Here is hoping yours is rich and full.'

'I have an idea, Dacier, that you're cynical about love,' Paula said, accepting a cigarette from his case, which glittered as the sun caught it and was monogrammed. Tina shook her head when it was offered and saw him quirk a blond eyebrow. His top lids sloped down at their outer edges adding a lazy look to his eyes, which swept over her face as he extended a lighter to the cylinder jutting from Paula's jade holder. The flame moved to the tip of his own cigarette and smoke jetted from the nostrils of his sculptured Latin nose.

'Are we not all cynical about love until it happens to us, Paula?' He lounged back in his chair, looking supremely at ease between the two women—as only a man with Latin blood can look. 'It is a fever against which few of us are immunized, and I do not expect to go through life without succumbing to its attack.'

'I thought Frenchmen were romantic about love,' Paula fenced.

'Not about love, *mon amie*. About marriage. When we marry we do not expect it to take care of itself, we know that it has to be worked at. It is within marriage that romance should constantly accelerate. To make a comparison, is there not more pleasure to be had out of a car which one has grown accustomed to handling; is it not more responsive, with an eager purr to it instead of a stiff reluctance to give of its best?'

'Dacier!' Paula put back her elegant head and trilled a laugh that was faintly piqued. 'You really are a brute! I might have expected you to quote "*Odi et amo*—I hate and I love", but never to compare women to cars. To you, then, a wife would be a possession, something to be run in until maximum performance is achieved?'

He grinned and shrugged in acknowledgment. 'I should hope, Paula, that to every man a wife is regarded as a possession, for to a man his possessions alone have real value. It is the nebulous things, the dreams, the pie in the sky, that belong to women.' He turned his audacious smile on Tina. 'Do you feel, *ma petite*, that to be a man's possession is not the ideal way to run a marriage? Do you wish to be at the driving wheel?'

Tina took a gulp of her drink and felt her head swim. 'I-I'm not the type to want more than to be a passenger, Mr. d'Andremont,' she replied. 'My happiness would lie in that, but naturally there are women who wish to share the driving seat.'

'To each man the right kind of woman, eh?' he smiled. 'We shop around for that, but we are not all fortunate enough to find our ideal—and then again our ideal is often snatched from beneath the nose by someone else.'

Even as Tina wondered if he was speaking personally, she saw Paula assume an idol-like tenseness and realized that for her the words had a double significance. Apprehension pierced Tina like a knife point—she could feel Paula's hate reaching out, touching her—

She jumped to her feet, then had to clutch at the table edge as the world spun alarmingly. 'I-I must be getting home,' she said. Her voice was distraite, and Dacier rose lithely out of his chair, looking concerned as Paula drawled:

'Tina isn't used to strong drink, *mon ami*. I'm meeting someone for lunch, so how about being a pet and running her home?'

'I shall be happy to do so.' He clasped a warm hand under Tina's elbow and drew her protectively against a body that felt firm as rock. They said good-bye to Paula and made their way out of the club and along the limestone walk to a sleek-finned convertible. He unlocked it and Tina slid in against the comfortable upholstery, raising grateful eyes to Dacier's face. 'I hope you haven't a date?' she said. 'I can take a cab—'

'You worry too much about other people, Mrs. Trecarrel,' he said, leaning on the door he had closed and watching her with narrowed eyes. 'Who taught you to be on edge all the time, like a little mouse? Not this husband of yours, I hope?'

'John?' She flushed and shook her head. 'John doesn't bully me.'

'That is just as well.' Dacier strode round the glistening bonnet and climbed into the car, large-limbed, smelling of the open air, platinum watch and golden hairs glinting on his wrist as he reached to the ignition and they shot away from the flower-bordered lawn of the club. Soon the ocean was beside them as they drove and Tina held her hat on her lap and let the breeze whip through her hair. She remembered John saying that there was a speed limit on the island, but it seemed that Dacier d'Andremont recognized few limits, whether they related to cars or people. But he slowed when there was a little more natural colour in Tina's cheeks, and she wondered at the way she felt more relaxed with him than she had ever felt with John. It was as though she had known him for years—comfortably as into an old shoe she had slipped into a strange intimacy with the man.

'You are too much a girl who likes to please people,' he remarked. 'You like them to smile and to be kind, but let me warn you that Paula Carrish is of the type who reserves her better side for the men of her acquaintance.'

'I know that,' Tina smiled ruefully, 'but she invited me to have a drink and I couldn't be rude and say no.'

'I think she had said something to upset you just before I joined you for a drink. Would it be a great impertinence if I asked what it was?'

Tina's fingers clenched on the straw brim of her hat, for how did she put into words the mood Paula had induced without making it sound like a sick fantasy to this high, wide and healthy man? 'My husband has been married before, as you probably know, Mr. d'Andremont, and Paula was showing me a picture of Joanna. I-I suppose I have a bit of a thing about her. She was hauntingly beautiful.'

'And you think she still haunts your husband, eh? Paula is encouraging you in this belief?'

'She doesn't have to encourage me. It happens to be true.'

Dacier's amber eyes flashed to meet Tina's. Then he said very deliberately: 'You, also, have beauty. Ah, but yes, *mignonne*, the very best kind that shines out from within. And you are so young, with few defences. There is a sweetness to it.' He smiled. 'You are very sweet, Tina.'

'You're rather nice yourself,' she wasn't too embarrassed by what he had said, only shot through with regret that she must hear such things from him and not from John. All the same they boosted her confidence, if they were true, and Dacier nodded his blond head when she smiled at him with doubt in her eyes.

'I find it fascinating the way you English girls are unaware of your charm,' he asserted. 'You have an air of retreat which is most enticing. Perhaps when I lose my heart it will be to an English girl . . . after all, my grandmother came from your country.'

When they reached Blue Water House, Tina invited him to stay for lunch, but he said he had a previous engagement and it was with a touch of regret that she watched him wave good-bye and sweep the convertible in an arc round the driveway plants. The powdered coral spattered and settled, a green parrot squawked in a tree and the lace-plants quivered. Tina, moving her hat like a fan, walked round the side of the house and in through the open glass doors of one of the ground floor rooms.

Coming in from the brilliant sunshine the room was dim, and she was half-way across it before she realized she was in the library and that John was at the big desk, a pen poised in his hand, gazing quizzically at her and waiting for her to notice him.

'H-hullo!' She stood poised like a startled crane, enormous eyes fixed on him, flaxen hair in disorder. She didn't move as he rose and came to her, but when his hands touched her shoulders she trembled from the love-ache that ran through her bones.

His hands tightened, registering, the tremor she couldn't control, then he let her go. 'Don't overdo the dashing about,' he said rather curtly. 'The trade winds cool the island to a certain extent, but you mustn't forget that our sun is a sub-tropical one.'

'I met Paula Carrish—didn't Topaz tell you?' Tina fought to sound casual, frustrated by his touch, longing for the kiss he had denied her. 'We ran into her as we were leaving the market and she invited me to have a drink at the Spindrift Club. She introduced me to Dacier d'Andremont—he's a rich Frenchman she was telling you about the other night. He's very nice. He gave me a lift home.'

'Tina,' John broke into a whimsical smile, 'I'm not asking for a list of your movements. I'm pleased you've had an enjoyable morning. That's what I want you to have, some fun.'

Fun! Tina moved away to his desk and picked up one of a pair of perfectly balanced bronze horses, running her fingers over the silk-smooth workmanship and reflecting that it hadn't been all fun that morning. She could still feel the smart of Paula's sly digs, and showing her that photograph of Joanna had been a brilliantly spiteful piece of strategy. She had ensured that from now on Joanna's vivid face would gaze back at Tina from every corner of Blue

Water House.

'When are you going to teach me to ride?' She spoke in an over-bright voice as she replaced the bronze horse, which she knew without being told was a piece of John's work.

'How about this afternoon, if you aren't feeling too beat from your shopping expedition?' He leant against a corner of his desk and surveyed the downbent curve of her profile and pale swing of her hair.

'It was amusing watching Topaz haggling with the various shopkeepers.' She glanced up and met with a breathless sense of shock the intense blue of his eyes. Lean and easy, he leant there, her husband, and yet a stranger. She had only to reach out a hand and it would have touched him, but her hands could not move, they were shackled by uncertainty and shyness. She knew in this moment that a wall of reserve was growing between herself and John and that they were both contributing to its construction. Fear and anger flared inside her and she wanted to batter it down before it cut them off completely from one another—but her hands stayed clenched at her sides, for already there was no sense of communication with John and she dreaded a rejection from him.

'I'd better go and freshen up for lunch,' she said, making for the door.

'You're forgetting your hat—here.' He whizzed it across and laughed unkindly when she missed catching it.

Upstairs she showered and changed into a tangerine blouse and a pair of white, flared pants. She brushed her hair and latched it back in a pair of white slides, then was turning to go downstairs when an imp of curiosity compelled her into the adjoining lounge and across to the door of John's room. She turned the handle and glanced in. It was a big room, untidy and lived-in. On his dressing-chest there were college and navy groups, a stud box in hide, a pair of ivory-backed brushes, a tobacco jar shaped like a Toby jug . . . but no personal photograph of Joanna. Not there or on the bedside table where a couple of books and a pipe jostled with a leather-bound clock and an attractive mounted photograph of Liza sitting astride her pony.

Tina could feel her heart pounding as she closed the door. She had found out that he did not sleep with Joanna's lovely face gazing at him, but it was a short-lived flicker of reassurance, for it was hardly likely in the circumstances that he would flaunt her in front of his second wife.

Wife? The word was farcical when applied to herself, she thought, pausing at the bend of the stairs to gaze from the rose window at the blue-green ocean and coral beach. If John were in love with her he'd want to make love to her. It was the rational thing to suppose, but it seemed that whatever transient attraction she'd had for him in England had vanished now he saw her against the background that had been so natural to Joanna.

She thrust her hands into the slant pockets of her pants and went on down the stairs. Liza called her name, then came sliding down the waxed banister rail, jolting to a halt against the carved post and swinging a long leg over it. They went into the dining-room together and a few minutes later were joined by John.

* * *

The next few days passed pleasantly enough, and Tina learned to do several things she had never dreamed of when living in Chorley with her aunt. She discovered the fun of horseback riding, sailing a catamaran, and reef fishing for amberjack. John even gave her one or two driving lessons, but he was rather an impatient teacher and she was relieved when he said she'd better get herself enrolled at a driving school before the car ended up with shattered gears. He grinned derisively as he spoke, and sparked her temper.

'We can't all be brilliant at things,' she flashed. 'I've never pretended to be anything but ordinary.'

His eyebrows reached for his hairline at her outburst, but he drove on without comment. His silence was eloquence enough for Tina; she was ordinary and he wasn't going to pretend otherwise. Her nails dug pits in her palms and she wished fiercely she had not gone to the Chorley headland that windy, fateful day in March . . . but inevitably there came a reversal of this wish when, the following morning, he wandered into her bedroom with his hair ruffled and a robe draped over his pyjamas, beguiling a share of her breakfast teapot. She had done away with tea-bags and her tea was now being brewed as it should be, in its natural state.

John sat beside her on her bed,

plundering triangles of toast and curls of butter, and it was all Tina could do not to launch herself into his arms and take whatever consequences resulted. But she wasn't a gambler by nature and she clung to what she had rather than risk it in a grand slam. She watched closely each move in the game and came to the conclusion that she played against a poker-face. John gave little away. He treated her in a kind enough fashion, but really she was what Paula Carrish had insinuated—a big sister for Liza.

Not that she minded Liza making up a threesome, for somehow her presence eased the faint tension that seemed to spring into life between John and herself when they were alone in the evenings. These hours together could have been so rich, she thought wistfully, but instead they passed in a separateness she knew no way of bridging. John would sit absorbed in sketches for the new piece of sculpture he was planning, while Tina lost herself in colourful tales of the Caribbean islands.

Great white moths fluttered round the lamps hanging in the veranda. Sprinklers watered the lawns and a fresh, moist scent mingled with that of the many blossoms, especially the frangipani, which had a peach-like fragrance that turned peculiarly bitter when the flower was cut from the tree. Tina, thinking it pretty, had arranged some branches in a vase, but the coral stars had quickly withered and when she had thrown them away the bitterness they exuded had saddened her. It seemed to her in her present hypersensitive state that love could go the way of the frangipani, which bloomed so richly only to die so bitterly. Even in its growth it was somehow symbolic, for the star-flowers and leaves clustered at the extremity of the branches, leaving the tree with a hollow heart. The sap, John had told her, was poisonous!

This particular evening, after coffee and cognacs, they sat in their usual separateness in cushioned cane chairs, the lamp above John flickering its light over his dark head and angular features. Absorbed in what he was doing, she knew he was totally withdrawn from an awareness of her. She watched him, shifting his pipe now and again, tapping his left thumb against the cleft in his chin, nodding to himself and adding another line or curve to the sketch he was working on. In a way it pleased Tina that she did not intrude on his working mood, that she was not an object of discord that sent him to the seclusion of his studio. This was the only real intimacy of her marriage, she realized, but the sort that usually came to a couple when their heady raptures had matured into a deeper-toned relationship.

Tina, only twenty-one and with the static of love sparking in her veins, wanted those heady raptures . . .

Grown restless, she put aside her book and went to the parapet of the veranda, where she leant on it and listened to the chirruping of the cicadas and occasional croak of a tree-frog. The palm trees rustled and between their fronds glinted the stars that seemed to mass into brooches against the dense velvet of the tropical sky. A shy little horn of a moon was piercing the velvet, the milky glow draining the touch of honey from Tina's skin and leaving her throat and arms moth-white against the blue of her dress.

She tensed and gripped the stone of the parapet as nuttily-sweet smoke drifted to her nostrils and John strolled over. 'Grand night, isn't it?' he murmured above her head. 'You could count the stars . . . is that what you're doing, Tina, or are you wishing on them?'

'There's a new moon,' she said. 'I've wished on that.'

'What for, I wonder?' She heard a faint catch in his voice. 'But I mustn't ask, of course, otherwise your wish won't come true.' He moved and leant an elbow on the parapet, facing her in the moon-glow. 'Are you superstitious, Tina?'

'About some things,' she admitted, thinking of the frangipani which dripped in a pale mass from a nearby tree, filling the air with its peachy tang. 'I know you men put more faith in down-to-earth realities, but think of the fun you're missing in not being able to believe that a pixie in your purse will bring you luck, and that when a frog's vest turns from gold to russet there will be rain.'

'I wish, Tina, that you could stay as disenchanted by life's realities as you are right now.' His face as he spoke wore an expression that baffled her, he seemed irritated and yet reluctantly amused. 'We all have to grow up some time, however, and I'm warning you that the situation between us is heading for a showdown. We should have had it before we got married, but there just wasn't time for heart-to-heart chats—' he paused, raking the pallor of her face with slitted blue eyes. 'You're frightened, aren't you?'

Terrified, she could have answered. He wanted one of two things of her, a loveless marriage or an annulment of the face. She . . . she wanted his love.

She watched him tap out his pipe against the edge of his hand, then thrust it into a pocket. One of his arms slipped round her and he held her quietly as he gazed down into the whispering garden. In a while he said: 'Liza's off to a birthday party tomorrow afternoon, isn't she?'

Tina nodded. 'She's looking forward to it. It's a pity this is such a wideflung neighbourhood and that she hasn't a next-door friend.'

'She has you until she returns to school.' He spoke rather dryly. 'Anyway, tomorrow afternoon I'm going to take you to Orange Coral Cay to meet an old friend of mine, Rachel Courtney. She lives on the cay and is quite a character. You'll like her.'

'Orange Coral Cay,' Tina repeated. 'What a colourful name for an island!'

'Mmmm.' He glanced down at her. 'Do you like Ste. Monique, Tina? Does it seem as romantic to you as on the day I told you about it? Or do you find that a closer acquaintance has dispelled the magic? Sometimes that happens, no matter how desperately we cling to the hope that it won't.'

Her heart shrank within her, for that surely was what had happened to him. He had hoped in England to recapture what he had once known with Joanna—instead he found himself robbed of his hope, disappointed in the young, callow thing he had so impetuously married. Tina could have wept, but tears would have given her away to him. He would be compassionate and mop her dry against his shoulder, but of all the things she craved from him, pity was the least of them. She therefore clung to her control and her pride as she assured him that she found Ste. Monique a lovely and interesting place.

She knew the minute she spoke that she sounded like a tourist on a visit, someone who expected to be leaving instead of staying. John gripped her shoulders and searched her face with eyes that seemed to burn with an impatience he was only barely controlling. 'Don't be stiff and polite with me, Tina,' he crisped. 'It's disconcerting . . . you make me feel that I've hurt you in some way without being aware of doing so. What are you sulking about? That spat in the car the other afternoon?'

'Oh, that!' She managed a laugh of dismissal. 'I'm used to being called incompetent.'

'I don't happen to think you incompetent, you little fool!' Now he was really angry, his lean features carved of it, his fingers bruising her shoulder bones. 'Snap out of this stupid habit of thinking yourself less than you are, and develop some self-esteem.'

'What on?' she asked, the stone of the parapet against her spine, the tormenting length and strength of John's body pressing hers. 'Do you think I don't know that when people look at me they're comparing me to Joanna and finding me a poor substitute? I have no beauty of face and form. I'm a novice at all the things she could do so well—' Then, unforgivably, prodded on by the devouring pain of his closeness of body and separateness of heart, she added wildly: 'You'd have done better to marry Paula. She's much more suitable in every way.'

He caught his breath, sharply, then as though he knew no other way to silence her, short of striking her, John ground her mouth to numbness beneath his. His arms crushed her ribs and she felt the frantic pounding of his heart against her. It was as though he wanted to kill her, and in a mindless panic she pushed, fought, gripped wildly a fistful of his hair as he swung her to the cushioned lounger. Desperately she tried to wrench free of his assaulting mouth, for not like this had she wanted him, in anger and reckless passion . . .

And yet of their own volition her fingers relaxed their straining grip on his hair and found his face. She felt the warm, moist skin, the pulse hammering madly beside his mouth .. dragged suddenly from hers as though something jerked him cruelly to his senses. She watched with wide, dazed eyes as he loomed to his feet, then turned blindly from her and shot down the steps into a thick wedge of shadow. His footfalls died away into the heart of the garden, and slowly a shudder of revulsion swept over Tina. Now he would hate her for what she had forced him to reveal . . . a hunger and an anguish connected with Paula Carrish!

With a hand holding a broken silk strap to her shoulder she made her way upstairs to her bedroom. She locked herself in, not out of trepidation but in case he came in to apologize and found her weeping her heart out in her pillows.

*　　　　*　　　　*

Last night's shattered emotions had jelled together into a thin protective skin, and Tina appeared for breakfast looking calm even if she didn't feel it. Liza was full of chatter, which seemed to ease the tension, and when the meal ended she hurried Tina away to help select a dress for the party that afternoon. It came out that a rather dishy boy was going to be there, and Tina, lending an ear to this tale of young love, was reminded of her own empty childhood and the things she had been unable to confide to her aunt.

Aunt Maud had not been an easy person to talk to, and from out of those childhood repressions had sprung Tina's present inability to tell John, simply and fearlessly, that she loved him. She shrank away from it more than ever since last night, for there had been no tenderness, nothing but a fierce hunger in his kisses and the way he had held her. He had triggered off responses in her because of her feeling for him, but in the clarity of daylight she knew that a consummation obtained from passion would not have brought them closer to each other. Certainly not a passion resulting from what he seemed to feel in a strange, bitter way for another woman!

Tina and the child finally settled on a dress, an apricot confection with ribbon trimming, then they went out to the garden to sit in a canopied couch-swing. The atmosphere was hammering with heat and Tina didn't want Liza over-exerting herself down on the beach, so to keep her amused she read aloud to her a couple of chapters of *The Coral Island*, a yarn she had loved herself as a child. She had lived in library books. They had opened up for her a warm, beckoning world where she had found excitement and escape from Maud Manson's harsh personality.

'You make it sound so real,' Liza said admiringly, when Tina grew thirsty and had orange drinks brought out to them. 'You made me go cold when you read that cave exploring bit, with the water gradually rising outside and the children looking at each other with big, scared eyes. Ooh, look, I've still got goosebumps!'

With her legs curled beneath her, Tina

sucked her orange juice through a straw. 'Make friends with books, Liza, and you'll never know what it is to be bored,' she advised. 'Pop records are great fun, but don't neglect all the best things, especially fine music and the splendid kind of art your father gives to the world.'

'Pops is clever, isn't he?' Liza swung the couch and crunched the cube of ice out of her drink. 'I bet I won't have his abilities when I grow up. Anyway, it isn't important for a girl to be as clever as a man, is it, Tina?'

'If she wants a career it helps, Liza. But it's much better to have a warm heart if a girl is more interested in marriage.'

'What about being nice-looking?' Liza asked. 'My friends at school say boys aren't interested in girls unless they're pretty.'

'I don't think that's strictly true,' Tina smiled. 'It must be nice to be pretty and admired, of course, but a bit on the empty side for a boy if there's nothing inside the colourful wrapping. I'd say most boys like a girl they can talk to as well as enjoy looking at.'

Liza hugged her knees against her chest and blinked her long, dark lashes as she thought this over. 'You're nice to talk to,' she informed Tina, then added: 'Everyone says my mother was beautiful, but I was so young when she died and I can't remember her at all. But I can remember my Cornish Nanna. Pops took me to England to see her when I was about six, just before she died. She was little and thin, like a pixie, with ever so many lines in her face. She told me to love Pops very much, but never to—to think I owned him or that he owned me. What did she mean, Tina?'

'That if we aren't careful, darling, we can make life a burden for the people we love. We can possess them, greedily, as we might a special toy or ornament, never wanting anyone else to touch them.' Tina curled an arm about Liza and gave her a squeeze. 'You love your father in the best way because you've been able to accept me as your stepmother. If you hadn't done so, then your love would have been the kind your grandmother was talking about. The selfish, clinging kind that strangles love in the other person.'

'I don't like that word stepmother. It's hard, with edges jutting out all over it, and it doesn't suit you one little bit.' Liza nuzzled against Tina's shoulder like an affectionate puppy, then drew back as Tina caught her breath in pain. 'Did I hurt you?' the child asked in alarm.

'No, it was just my bra strap digging in me.' Tina drew the dark head back against her shoulder, which under her dress was marked in several places by plum-dark bruises. They had shocked her when she had seen them that morning, the tangible evidence of John's violence last night, put there when he had forced her to quiescence on the lounger in the veranda. She hadn't known that John was capable of giving way like that, and it had been terribly late when she had finally heard him enter his room. Just once had their eyes met across the breakfast table, a cool, withdrawn expression in his which had chilled Tina's heart. But towards the end of the meal he had said: 'Don't forget we're going to see Rachel Courtney this afternoon.'

She took that as a tacit agreement that they would forget last night. Pretend that agonizing scene had not occurred. Oh, God, who was John kidding? He must know as well as she that things had now taken a turn for the worse between them.

A bird settled on a branch of a nearby magnolia tree, and Tina, watching it perched there in a wondering, uncertain way, felt that it typified her own position at Blue Water House. She, too, trembled on the verge of flight though she longed to settle down and build her nest.

That afternoon when Joe nosed the motor-launch through the reef, choppy little waves were dancing on the water, while the air shimmered with heat. For coolness Tina wore an apple-green halter dress, the straps thankfully wide enough to conceal her bruised shoulder. A coolie hat shaded her eyes. John, smoking a cheroot beside her, was in cream tropical drill. It threw into relief his dark Cornish looks and made him seem rather foreign.

'Say, Joe,' he suddenly called out, 'is there a storm building up?'

'Reckon there is, boss.' Joe scanned the sky with his seaman's eyes. 'What time it start I cain't figger. You want me to turn back?'

'No, we'll carry on to Miss Courtney's place. She's expecting us.' John glanced down at Tina. 'If the weather turns dodgy, the Macraes will keep Liza overnight, so don't go getting jumpy.'

Her hands had clenched on the rail at the word storm, and it was just like John's sharp eyes to spot the action. 'It's natural for me to worry about her,' she replied.

'And maybe about being marooned on the cay with me, eh?' There was raw scorn in his voice, mockery in his eyes when she braved a meeting with them. 'Auntie should have told you the facts of life, my sweet, not left you to pick them up, probably out of some darn novel.'

'I don't know what you mean,' she gasped.

'Oh, come!' Cheroot smoke jetted down his nostrils. 'What the devil was all the melodrama about last night if you weren't scared stiff? You fought me like a little wildcat, then scampered away to your room and shot the bolt on your door. I recall that I advised you to do so, but the thing that wasn't necessary was for you to throw Paula in my teeth.'

'I-I'm sorry about that,' she whispered, her throat thick with pain and terror at the way they were sinking deeper into a morass of misunderstanding. 'John—'

'Yes?' His eyes, cold and hard, rested on her triangular face beneath the drooping brim of her hat. A soft coating of natural honey showed off her woodsmoke eyes—she seemed more adult this afternoon and strangely attractive—but John looked at her as though at someone he didn't particularly like any more.

It was a look that sent her shrinking into her shell. 'I-I wish things could be different between us,' she managed, without a scrap of confidence to give the words life and meaning. They trailed away and were lost in the sound of the sea and the throb of the launch's motor.

'I wish it, too,' he drawled, flicking ash over the rail. 'It's a pity they can't be, but for now let's put a cheerful face on our deplorable mistake. We owe that much to Liza. When she returns to school on Monday we'll decide on a course of action.'

He strolled away to speak to Joe, leaving Tina encased in her private pain. Alone there at the rail she really grew up and knew she would never be a child again. The strange thing was, her love for John had not died; it had grown. It was now a woman's love, intense, and strong enough to bear a parting from him if that was his wish. She watched the flurry of the spray and listened to the hiss of the waves as they slithered and scattered before the hull of the launch. Ahead of them a small island was coming into view and she tensed as John came back to her side and informed her that they were approaching their destination. Once they were past a fretted coral reef, there were colourful native catamarans dancing on the aquamarine water streaked with violet, and gri-gri trees and tufted palms rising from a beach of crushed tangerine coral. Tina saw a scattering of palm-thatched houses on the cay, and they berthed to quite a welcoming committee of chocolate-coloured urchins.

With a grin John turned to Joe and told him to toss over the big fancy sweet tin which Tina had thought was a present for Miss Courtney. John handed the tin to the biggest of the children and told him to share out the sweets, had a few words with some of the adults who were unloading fish off the catamarans, and then piloted Tina along a path that wound between a grove of tamarind trees that eventually opened to reveal a fairly large, palm-thatched house with a broad timeworn sun porch and a front garden in which grew large Shasta daisies, bright cannas, and pink and blue hortensias.

John opened the gate and down the garden path, formed of colourful pieces of stone and tile set in cement, came dashing a cream and cocoa basset-hound. Grinning all over his comical face, he leapt at John and whined a lovelorn greeting, then he trotted round Tina, decided he liked what he saw and thumped his tail against her legs.

'Johnny Trecarrel, how are you!' boomed a voice, and Tina glanced up from patting the dog to find a woman advancing towards them down the path. She was quite elderly, triple-chinned, and jangling with necklets and bracelets. Flowered georgette floated around her and she had the widest, friendliest smile Tina had seen in a long while.

'I'm fine, Rachel!' John took the hand she held out and gave it a firm shake. 'You're looking well yourself.'

'Can't grumble, dear boy. The old indigestion plays me up now and again, but I like to eat, and when you reach my age there isn't much else left to do.' She swung her glance to Tina and took her in from the apple-green braces over her slender young shoulders to her small, sandalled feet. 'This is your bride, eh, Johnny?'

'Yes, this is Tina.' There was no more of that wounding mockery in his voice, and he even smiled down briefly into Tina's eyes. In front of Rachel Courtney, who was obviously an old and valued friend, he wanted them to appear a normal, honeymooning couple. 'Honey, meet Rachel, one of the nicest people in the West Indies,' he said.

'How do you do, Miss Courtney?' Tina held out her hand, which was taken in two big ringed hands and soundly squeezed.

'We don't go in for ceremony on Orange Coral Cay,' boomed Rachel. 'Call me by my first name, dear child, it makes me feel young. H'm, you're surprisingly young, aren't you, and a bit on the timid side? Don't know what I was expecting, someone modern and flashy, I suppose.'

'I thought you knew me better than that, Rachel,' John laughed.

'Ah, but you're at a funny age, dear boy, and likely to get entangled with a smart, brittle piece now you've got silver in your hair. Don't think because I never got off the shelf that I know nothing about men.' Again she looked Tina over and commented, with a shake of her grey head: 'When I think of the lumber I was forced to wear when I was a girl—how times have changed. All the goods are on display these days.'

'Yes, now we know what we're getting for our money—though it's true we can still be fooled,' John added, near to Tina's ear as he bent to give the basset-hound an affectionate cuff.

She winced at the dig, and as she followed their hostess into the sun porch she wondered at her own ability to love so deeply a man who had never really cared for her. Gone was that transient affection she had aroused in him back in England. Shattered her dream of turning it to love.

CHAPTER SEVEN

A FAN purred steadily in the sun porch, but the air wasn't cooled, it was just circulated heat. Tina cradled a long glass of an exotic concoction squeezed from passion-fruits and chilled by fragments of diamond-bright ice; her rattan chair faced towards the garden so that she didn't have to look at John each time she raised her eyes. Through the tamarind trees glinted a triangle of blue-green ocean—tormentingly blue-green—and she longed to plunge to her ear-tips in water and cool off her perspiring skin. Her shoulder throbbed, her heart ached, and it was sheer willpower that prodded her to conversational efforts.

There was no getting away from the fact that she liked Rachel Courtney, who possessed a happy quality of making people feel at home, but this particular afternoon Tina wasn't in the mood for anyone's company except her own. She wanted to wallow in the misery that locked her as palpably as the heat the stormy sun was shedding over everything.

The plants and flowers stood motionless as plastic creations, while lizards lay on the crazy paving like petrified images. The basset-hound was now sprawled in the shade beside John's chair, his jowl propped on one of the large sandals. John had slung his jacket over the porch rail, and as he chatted with Rachel he looked entirely relaxed—also very attractive—in a short-sleeved tan silk shirt.

'Has Liza taken to her new mother?' Rachel wanted to know.

'Amazingly so,' John drawled, while Tina numbly wondered what the child's reaction would be when her 'new mother' departed from Ste. Monique.

'I hope the pair of you have plans to give your Liza a sister or brother,' Rachel went on blithely. 'Having had my own life rather messed up by being an only child, I'm on the side of sensible-sized families.' The ringed fingers played with a rope of crystals. 'As Johnny knows, Tina, I wouldn't leave my ailing father long ago to marry a Canadian rancher, the only man who ever mattered to me. I've never put all the blame on my father for the sacrifice I made, but I've often regretted the fact that I had no sisters or brothers who could have eased my father's loneliness had I married. His health wouldn't permit him to travel at that time and he dreaded being left on his own. Ah well, it does no good to rake over dead ashes. It's best to let them sift away with the winds of time—but now and again a spark blows back to bring a tear or two.'

Then Rachel broke into a cheery smile and gave Tina's knee a squeeze. 'You must fill Blue Water House with some lively youngsters, my dear. The place has stood empty and waiting too long.'

Tina caught her bottom lip between her teeth—the lip that was still tender from those ruthless kisses last night—and couldn't help glancing at John for his reaction to what Rachel had said. His face was dark and impassive, his blue eyes resting upon her a cool, cynical look that made her feel awful, as though she had betrayed him. Yet surely the betrayal had been his? When he had hauled her into his arms, he had been driven not by a need of her, his wife, but by a hunger for the woman whose name he had locked between their lips during those savage kisses.

Savage . . . yet thrilling to remember, tightening the nerves under Tina's rib-cage so that she caught her breath. If only she could have felt that he was kissing her like that because it was *she* who charged him to such emotion . . .

Why had he not married Paula? Could he possibly suspect that she had had something to do with Joanna's death? How terrible for John if true! Tina moistened her dry mouth with her drink, then set aside the glass because her wrist was shaking, her skin clammy. The cocoa plants, the poincianas and hortensias, were surging together into a blaze of colour, while the voices beside her were fading away down a tunnel. As she realized that she was coming over faint, she did the usual panicky thing—rose to her feet. At once the gaily patterned porch floor wavered towards her, but before she felt its impact a pair of arms closed strong and hard around her. A voice spoke her name in a tone of alarm, then she went out like a light.

She revived on a bed, the ammonia of smelling-salts stinging her nostrils, and the bolster of Rachel's bosom supporting her. 'Wh-what a silly thing to do,' she murmured.

'Rest easy, dear child,' came Rachel's soothing voice, 'and take another sniff or two at my smelling bottle. There, are you beginning to feel a little better?'

'Yes, th-thanks.' Never in her life before had Tina passed out like that, and she felt shaken and scared. Rachel gave her a drink of water, then went over to the window and lowered the blind.

'You aren't used to the kind of heat we're getting today, dear child,' she said, but as she returned to the foot of the big bedstead, with its tall posts surmounted by carved pineapples, she was looking at Tina with twinkles in her eyes. 'You're a bride, of course, and I could go jumping to a more pleasant conclusion. Is there any chance that you threw that faint because you're starting a family?'

Tina shook her head in such an emphatic fashion that Rachel raised her eyebrows.

'Well, you know best, my dear. Not nervous about producing an infant, are you?'

'Not in the least, Rachel.' To hide what might be showing in her eyes, the longing for such an occurrence and the pain of knowing it was not to be, Tina turned to up-end a pillow, against which she rested her languid body. She didn't like this lassitude, for though she wasn't physically tough, she had a healthy constitution. It was doubtless the heat combined with emotional worry which had caused her to flake out. 'Did John carry me up here?' she asked.

Rachel nodded and re-seated herself on the bed beside Tina. 'Have you anything on your mind you'd like to get off it?' she demanded frankly. 'I know Johnny can be close-mouthed when he likes, and if there are things he won't talk about, then I might be able to provide a few answers. It would be only human of you, Tina, to be curious about his first wife.'

Tina's fingers clenched the lace bedspread, then in a driven way she broke into a question. 'Was her death an accident, Rachel?'

'You want me to be quite frank?'

'Please!'

'I think a spat with her cousin led to her death.'

'Oh, Rachel!' Tina shuddered from head to toe, and clearly as though she had been on that yacht she saw Joanna leap over the side, driven to her premature death by things Paula had revealed about her association with John. By a cruel quirk of fate he had been on the beach that morning and he had seen his wife plunge into the sea. He must have known that Paula was the indirect cause of her death, yet he had protected her and kept quiet. His reason for doing so was so apparent that Tina could hardly bear the torment of it.

'Let the dead ashes sift away, my dear,' Rachel advised, pressing a large, warm hand over Tina's left one, white-knuckled and winking its rubies as it clenched and unclenched. 'Help Johnny to find a fresh happiness.'

But he made his own past misery, Tina clamoured to reply. He let himself get tangled up with Paula . . .

'I knew Joanna well,' Rachel said quietly. 'She was vividly attractive and at the same time she seemed helplessly appealing. She was the type a young and artistic man would be drawn to, and she was desperately attached to him. Love is always a precarious state of heart and mind when it's a total dependence upon another person for every scrap of joy and happiness. It can eat away at the fabric of marriage, and if Johnny's first marriage went wrong, the blame can't be laid entirely at his door. A man gives half of himself to his work, the other half to his wife, and the wisest women accept this. Some are not so wise.'

'Joanna wasn't?' Tina murmured.

'Unfortunately not, dear child.'

'A-and because of that he—he had an affair with Paula?' The angles of Tina's face sharpened as she put the question that must now receive an answer.

Rachel shrugged her heavy shoulders and pursed her lips. There was a silence filled with the cat-purr of a fan and the thudding of Tina's heart. 'I've seen a lot of life, my dear,' Rachel said, 'and I've learned not to judge the mistakes of others. In one way or another we pay for them, and if Johnny ever felt anything for Paula Carrish he has paid for it and put it out of his life. Passion is an exotic but quick-dying flower. Love is the evergreen, if treated with a care that does not smother it, and it goes on and on, come rain or shine. If that's how you care for Johnny, then don't let anything crush it out of existence.'

'W-what if he doesn't care quite so much for me?' Tina asked.

Rachel's eyes searched the pale, troubled face framed in the bamboo-straight hair. 'Love often springs from need, my dear, and Johnny must need you, otherwise he wouldn't have married you.' The big, kindly woman patted Tina's cheek, then heaved herself to her feet. 'Have a little rest, it will do you good.'

After she had gone from the big, dim room with its smell of crushed lavender, old black walnut, and sun-dried linen, Tina lay in her lassitude staring at the ceiling, the faint breeze from the fan cooling her throat and forehead. Could Rachel be right about John needing her? Was there still hope for them, even now, when they were poised on the razor-edge of a parting? He must care about hurting Liza, and to deprive her of the mother she so obviously needed would be sheer heartlessness. And he wasn't heartless. He had loved Joanna until her possessiveness had driven him from her.

Love, surely the most painful and

inexplicable emotion in the world. Something you couldn't grasp yet tangible enough to stab the heart as it was stabbing Tina's right now. Sometimes stronger than you were, so that you hurt the very people you would die for.

John had known why Joanna had wanted to die. He had tried to stop it from happening, and afterwards he had protected Paula, but in so doing he had also protected his wife's name. If she had leapt intentionally from that yacht to the rocks and the sea, then she had taken her own life. Better, far better, to call it an accident and not let Liza grow up with the stigma of a maternal suicide hanging over her.

Tina's breast rose on a shaky sigh. In an agony of apprehension at what John intended doing; tearless and yet grieving, she drifted off to sleep.

She awoke a couple of hours later to find the dark bedroom lit by flashes of lightning. Thunder roared and she could hear the pounding of tropical rain. So the storm had broken, which meant that John wouldn't attempt the crossing back to Ste. Monique until the weather quietened down . . .

Then Tina sat up sharply. Unless he had

gone home without her, leaving her in Rachel's charge! Maybe until Monday, when he would return with her baggage and an air-flight ticket! Nerves leaping, she slipped off the bed and was shown the door by a flare of steel-bright lightning. She turned the knob, stepped out on to the landing, and then stood motionless, relief nearly stopping her heart as a tall figure came towards her carrying an oil-lamp.

'I was just coming to see how you were feeling.' John was now quite close and gazing down at her with concerned eyes. 'You still look washed out.'

'I'm all right,' she said. 'The heat was a bit too much for me, that's all. The air feels cooler now it's started to rain.'

He nodded and still scanned her in the leaping light of the lamp in his hand. Her hair was in disarray from her prolonged nap, and she looked small, bemused and fragile outlined against the dark wood of the door. John put out his other hand and, inadvertently, touched the shoulder he had bruised with angry fingers. Tina winced before she could stop herself, and, his eyes gone narrow, he deliberately slipped the strap of her dress and bared her discoloured skin.

'My doing?' His voice was made even harsher by a roll of thunder.

'I—I bruise easily,' she managed, putting up a hand and covering the marks. 'How long has it been storming?'

'About an hour—look, Tina, I didn't mean to hurt you—'

'I know.' Her throat moved painfully as she swallowed the lump that rose to it. 'I made you furious with my—my silliness last night. You're my husband. You have rights—'

'Rights!' He ground out the word. 'God, the way we abuse them! I scared you sick, and all day it's been on my conscience. I said things coming here that were mean and uncalled-for. Tina,' his fingers played with the ends of her hair, 'if you want to go away on Monday, then it's okay by me. A marriage without love forces you to do nothing that you find—repellent.'

The blood seemed to drain from Tina's heart as he said this, and she clutched wildly at her only valid excuse for begging a reprieve. 'Liza would be so hurt if I went away,' she exclaimed.

'You want to stay for Liza's sake, eh?' A brief smile cut lines in his face, but his eyes in the lamplight looked tired and sardonic.

'You've grown to care for her, haven't you?'

'Very much.' Relief seeped back and warmed Tina's voice, lit a brightness in her eyes. 'I didn't enjoy much of a childhood myself and Liza's become a sort of compensation for that. We—need each other, I think.'

She held her breath and waited for him to say that he, too, needed her, but instead he tweaked her hair and said in a dry voice: 'You don't have to look at me with such big and apprehensive eyes, Tina. If you stay at Blue Water I shan't expect you to make any sacrifices.' He paused, and she was about to break into speech when he left her dumb by adding: 'There are compensations for the taking on Ste. Monique, and I'll not starve for diversions. Now let's go down before Rachel comes dragging up to find out what's keeping us. We're dining here, by the way. It would be madness to risk going home in the launch while this storm is blowing.'

Tina preceded him down the rather narrow stairway on legs that felt they didn't belong to her. How could she help but guess what he had meant—that there was always a compensation for him in the seductive form of Paula Carrish!

* * *

Over a pot of China tea, without milk because it spoiled the smoky flavour, Rachel said she was delighted at the onset of the storm because it meant that Tina and John would now be sharing her usual lonely dinner.

An hour later she was beaming as she came bustling into the bedroom where Tina was combing her hair after a refreshing bath. Adjoining this room was a dressing-slot where John was tidying himself up. 'Have you ever worn a sari, dear child?' Rachel wanted to know.

Tina surveyed the long silk slip and length of opalescent shantung which hung over her hostess's arm. 'Why, no,' she said, looking intrigued. 'I think they're very pretty.'

'I can't lend you a dinner-gown of mine, it would look like a tent,' Rachel announced, 'so I'm going to show you how to wear a sari. You have exactly the figure for it, a pert little bosom and a boyish bottom. Game, my child, to give that husband of yours a nice surprise?' She lowered her voice and winked at the adjoining door.

Tina met Rachel's eyes and found it impossible to spoil this kindly woman's fun by refusing to let herself be dolled up. With a smile of acquiescence she rose from the dressing-table bench and came over to finger the glimmering shantung. 'How lovely! Is it the genuine article?' she asked.

'Absolutely. I lived in India when I was a girl. My father was a Government official there and that's where he picked up the bug that ruined his health. I've always liked warm climates, that's why I came to live here when he died. Now off with your dress, and I'll show you how those wonderful-looking Indian girls make themselves even more attractive.'

Rachel's rather primitive electricity had failed owing to the storm, and the bedroom in which Tina dressed was lit by a couple of oil-lamps. It could have been their leaping golden light that added a touch of mystery to her appearance, for when she was finally arrayed in the sari she found herself gazing into the mirror at a sylph-like stranger. A pulse hammered in her throat, for the exotic garment certainly did something for her. It went with her high cheekbones, strangely coloured eyes, and pale hair whirled into a cone-shaped pleat.

'Very nice,' Rachel murmured, straightening a fold of the sari. 'Do you like yourself?'

Tina would have been very unfeminine if she hadn't liked the reflection at which she was gazing. 'That saying about fine feathers certainly applies to me,' she laughed, a hand against the excited pulse in her throat.

'Most females look the better for a bit of razzle-dazzle,' Rachel chuckled. 'It was Oscar Wilde who said that women's styles may change but their designs remain the same.'

'What designs am I supposed to have?' Tina murmured.

'I think we both know that without having to put it into words.' Rachel gently pressed the shoulder bearing the bruises she had refrained from remarking on. 'You need a necklace, dear child. I have exactly the thing in my room, so hang on while I fetch it.'

She left Tina alone in the big lamplit room. The smell of the oil blended with the haunting aroma of old wood, while the ticking of the clock mingled with the stormy threshing of palm fronds beyond the curtained window. Tina couldn't hear John in the adjoining room, so she assumed he had gone downstairs. What would he say when he saw her dressed up like this? Would he be amused? More than likely.

Her hostess came bustling back with the promised necklace, which she clasped about Tina's neck. They were opals, scintillating with colour against the pale skin of Tina's throat. They certainly added the finishing touch to her exotic appearance, but she couldn't help wondering if it was true what people said about opals that they were unlucky.

She went downstairs with Rachel, dressed in an old-fashioned lace gown with a velvet flower pinned at her waist, and they found John awaiting them in the sitting-room, where the lamplight cast a cosy glow over the dining-table set with Rachel's best china and glassware. A branched candelabrum formed the centrepiece, old-fashioned and lovely with holders shaped like daffodil cups.

John lifted an eyebrow at Tina as he rose from a wicker lounger. 'Well, well, this is a surprise!' he drawled.

She broke into a shy smile, while the sari whispered as she walked across the colourful sisal rugs. She stood before her husband in a pose of unconscious grace, the lines of the gown flowing like opal-tinted water over the limbs of a naiad. 'Rachel's idea,' she said. 'Do you like it?'

He walked right round her, looking amused but not in an unkind way. 'It certainly brings out hidden facets of your personality, my child. You're quite stunning.'

Her breath caught in her throat, for he sounded as though he really meant the compliment. But she had to go carefully, treading with infinite care on the thin ice that still shimmered between them. She performed a graceful salaam. 'I live only to please my master,' she dared to murmur.

A quick smile tugged at the edge of his mouth. 'At this moment, Tina, I'm almost tempted to believe you.'

Rachel stood watching the pair of them, ringed hands clasped just below her bosom, obviously as pleased as Punch at the transformation she had wrought in Tina. 'What a pity Western women are losing their love of the exotic,' she said. 'The men of the East would never tolerate jeans, sweaters, and those ugly quilted things called anoraks.'

In that cosily lit room, with the rain beating down hard outside, dinner was an enjoyable and tasty meal. With their coffee they had a Chartreuse the amber of cat's eyes, which Rachel said she had been saving for just such an occasion as this one.

'I believe I still have some of Father's cigars in a cedarwood box I keep in the sideboard—ah, yes!' Rachel emerged rosy and beaming from the bowels of the cupboard and examined the contents of the box. 'Here you are, Johnny. Light up and envelop us in clouds of Havana smoke.'

He obliged, settling back in the candleglow, the end of his cigar pulsing orange as he drew on the rich brown cylinder. The storm had blown itself out and through the reed blind filtered a moist, tangy breeze. Tina, at ease among cretonne cushions, her eyelids weighted by two glasses of dinner wine and the delicious Chartreuse, floated on the dreamy melody of the record Rachel had placed on her gramophone. *Poor Butterfly*, the song was called. Poor pretty thing, who had loved a man who belonged to another woman!

'You can't beat the old tunes,' Rachel said, tapping her foot in time to it. 'This was all the go when I was a girl. To look at me now, round as a barrel, you'd never believe that I was one of the favourite dancing partners at the military hops out in Bombay years ago. Do you like to dance, Tina?'

'I've only ever done so in the privacy of my bedroom, holding a pillow for a partner,' Tina smiled, looking at Rachel but aware of John's eyes upon her profile.

'Tina had a rather restricted upbringing,' he drawled. 'She should have had someone like you, Rachel, to mother her when her parents died.'

'What fun we'd have had, dear child,' Rachel beamed. 'Most women are born with the urge to produce an infant, and caring for someone else's is the next best thing. Still, we're friends now and you must come across to the cay as often as you can. Johnny will let Joe bring you in the launch.'

'May I borrow Joe and the launch now and again?' Tina asked her husband.

'Of course, honey. I want you to make my buddies your friends.' He rose from his chair with a lazy stretch, then gave his left leg a rub as though it ached a bit.

'D'you still get trouble with that leg after all this time?' Rachel eyed him with concern.

'It's the damp,' he shrugged. 'Nothing more than the kind of nag you get from a tooth that doesn't like sugar.'

'It was a miracle you kept that leg,' Rachel said gruffly.

He nodded casually, but it was evident he had no intention of discussing the matter, for he turned to Tina and suggested that she change out of the sari. 'We ought to be getting home,' he added.

'You'll stay as you are, dear child.' Rachel smiled. 'The sari is yours—ah, but I insist! You look pretty as paint in it and there's nothing to stop you wearing it for private, romantic evenings at Blue Water. Now I'll get you a Kashmir shawl to wear on the walk down to the beach, and put your sun-dress into a bag.'

She bustled out of the room, and Tina drifted to the sideboard on which stood various Indian brasses and also one of the prettiest ornaments Tina had ever seen, a little silver birch tree with a unicorn tied to it. As she gave an exclamation of delight and picked it up, John came over and regarded it with her. 'I believe Rachel's Canadian gave her that many years ago,' he said. 'A unicorn is symbolic of the elusiveness of happiness, and for a man it is most often tied to the delicate form of a woman, which the silver birch symbolizes. The workmanship is beautiful, isn't it?'

He touched it and, purposely or not, had both arms around Tina in so doing. As she stood there, her shoulders against his chest, her heart beating fast, she knew that such a moment had to be grasped quickly before it eluded her and was lost. She turned into his arms. They were slack around her as he gazed straight down into her eyes and she nearly died of suspense and hope in the seconds that ticked away between them. Then, brushing casually at her hair, he said she looked tired, and her emotions that had been up on tiptoe sank down and she replaced Rachel's love-token and withdrew from contact with John. She removed the opals from around her neck with a tiny shiver.

Rachel returned with a fringed silk shawl which she swung around Tina's shoulders. She said good night to them on the veranda, and as she kissed Tina's cheek, John having loped ahead down the steps, she whispered: 'Don't let go of your dreams as easily as I did, dear child. Love is worth many sacrifices, especially the sacrifice of pride.'

Tina knew what Rachel meant, that if she wanted John she must shut her mind to the past and work towards the future. That she must give and in the giving hope to reap.

'I'll come again soon, Rachel,' she promised huskily.

'I shall look forward to seeing you, Tina. Good night, my dears! Safe crossing.'

'Good night, Rachel!' John called out, then holding Tina's arm he was walking with her along the path that wound between the damp, rustling tamarinds. The storm had passed right away and the night was strangely quiet, the stars glinting washed and bright through the fronds of the tall trees. They left the grove behind them, and as they walked down the beach Tina thought of Tennyson's 'Wet sands marbled by moon and cloud.' The scene was mysterious, the silvery ocean rippling round the lacing of the coral reef, and there at the rail of the launch the immense figure of Joe clamly awaiting them.

'Dat sure one humdinger of a storm, missus.' His teeth glimmered in the moonlight as he helped Tina aboard. John unhitched the launch from a bollard and leapt over the side, growling a cuss word under his breath that told Tina his leg was still playing him up.

'How's everything with your cousins on the cay, Joe?' he inquired.

'Dat Millicent got her hair straightened out, an' does she look a scarecrow!' Joe chortled richly as he started the motor. 'What we do with de womenfolk, boss? Ain't day everlastin' up to tricks?'

'You can say that again,' John laughed, and Tina glanced round from the rail to find him looking directly at her, a dark eyebrow quirked mockingly.

* * *

Tina and John took Liza back to school and stayed a couple of days in attractive Barbados. It was an extremely British island, Tina discovered, fertile and with an air of placid security. They stayed at a hotel set in a garden of purple moonflowers and scarlet hibiscus, above a bay where the colourful flying-fish fleets came in. Tina thought it a crime that these pretty, winged fish should be caught for eating, but she had to admit, when John scoffed her out of her prejudicc, that thcy made a delicious meal. Tina swam with John at Lover's Lagoon, where the sun shafting into the water revealed a rainbow of colours, and for the first time she saw his badly scarred thigh when they lay resting on a beach that was pink and delicate as a girl's blush.

The scar was jagged and wide, deeply indented in the hard flesh. Tina wanted to put gentle fingers against it. She wanted so much to get close to him with her new knowledge of herself as an adult woman, but he had assumed a companionable attitude towards her that in its own way was curiously soothing and serene. For now she thought it best to let things drift on this tide of calmness, aware that undercurrents would surge when they were ready.

She, too, would be ready, she vowed. Paula Carrish was not going to get a second chance to spoil John's life.

She listened to the lazy lullaby of the ocean that rippled over their feet, and gazed through drowsy lashes at the blue sky speckled with fleecy puff-ball clouds. Her flaxen hair lay in strands on the sand, sun-drained seaweed John had called it a moment ago. She smiled to herself and felt his toes playing with hers under the silky caress of the surf.

That evening they went into Bridgetown and dined at the Starlight Room, a rooftop restaurant shaded by palms and with a throbbing Bajun band. John wore tropical dinner clothes and looked, in Tina's opinion, the most distinguished man in the restaurant. A glint in his eye whenever he spoke to her informed her that she, too, was worth a second glance in the white lace dress that set off his pearls. It was the enticing number Gaye Lanning had persuaded her to buy, which left her shoulders bare to the cleft between her breasts and showed the slender length of her legs, honey-toned enough not to need tights, her small feet arching into silver shoes with twisted heel straps and high, slim heels. Her satin trench coat lay over the back of her chair, red as the lipstick she wore this evening.

'Is it true you've only ever danced with a pillow in your arms?' John asked, smiling lazily over the rim of his wine glass.

She nodded, one of her silver shoes tapping the floor to the rhythm of the Bajun band. Happiness tingled like an elusive caress.

'We'd better remedy that,' John said. 'I think the wonky leg is fit enough to give you a few whirls, though I was never all that much of a hoofer.' He rose and circled the table to her and next moment was leading her on to the floor. He enfolded her in his arms, then she felt his hand at her waist, pressing her to the crispness of his white tuxedo.

They most certainly wouldn't have won a prize for that foxtrot, but Tina floated on a cloud and enjoyed every moment of it. 'I can't believe that you are here, so close and near,' crooned the Bajun girl at the mike. 'It can't be wrong, it must be right, so, tonight, hold me tight . . .'

Upon leaving the restaurant they took a starlight drive in an open-top gig, the horse's hooves clopping on a quiet road winding under the moon that was now full and golden. They might have been real honeymooners, Tina thought, and wondered if John was thinking the same, for when they arrived at their hotel he suggested a stroll among the moonflowers before they turned in. 'These few days have been good, eh?' he said. 'Barbados is always unspoiled—unchanging.'

'I've enjoyed every moment of our stay,' she agreed.

He stopped walking where a lily pool

shimmered, then very gently he framed Tina's face in his hands and raised it to the filtering moonbeams. Her limbs and her body seemed to go fluid, and she was prepared to believe in this moment that if fondness was all he had to give, then she could take it and not cry for the stars. 'Ah, Tina,' he murmured, and though his cheek came to rest against her soft, swathing hair, he didn't try to kiss her. Her heartbeats grew slower and she wondered numbly if here in the scented night phantoms were haunting him. Had he visited Barbados with Joanna? Had they stood like this among the moonflowers? Leaves rustled as though a ghostly hand stirred them, and Tina shivered uncontrollably . . .

'Let's go in,' John said, and he moved away from her, leaving her cold, lost, knowing only that something tormented him.

They went home the following day, and almost immediately John started to work in his studio. This was quite a special retreat, with a domed glass roof shedding lots of light down into the room which was always strangely cool, maybe because of the moist clay and the various finished and unfinished pieces of sculpture grouped in corners. Tina was naturally curious about the procedure of John's work, and though he showed her how to build a figure from the inside with rolled fingers of clay, he liked to be alone unless he was using a model and because of the sustained concentration involved in creating something from a shapeless mass she had to give him time, when he emerged from his studio each evening, to switch from a lonely, creative mood into a relaxed and sociable one.

There would be an endearing air of abstraction about him when they met in the salon for a sundowner, his hair would be ruffled and sticky from the clay he had been handling, and there would be pipe ash on his slacks. Evidently there were moments when inspiration eluded him, for one afternoon he spent hours carving Tina a little pearwood ornament. It was Psyche with tiny wings sprouting from her delicate shoulders, a gem in its detail and its appeal to the imaginative streak in Tina. She stood it on her dressing-table and wondered, with a catch at her heart, whether John associated her with the fairy-like Psyche who had been enamoured of Cupid.

These days at Blue Water House weren't

unhappy ones. Shopping with Topaz one morning she spotted a face she knew, and next moment was smiling up into the hazel-green eyes of Ralph Carrish. 'How come you haven't been to see me yet?' he demanded.

She had been putting off a visit to him because of the necessity of seeing Paula at the plantation bungalow, but when Ralph informed her, in a casual tone of voice, that he would be alone the following afternoon, she agreed to have tea with him.

'I'll lay on a spread and a tour, so don't go letting me down.' He nipped her fingers in friendly warning and asked Topaz how her children were getting along.

'Dey fine, Mr. Ralph.' Topaz flashed her handsome teeth at him and displayed not a sign of the antagonism Tina had noticed when they had run into his sister the other week.

Ralph bade them good-bye, and as they proceeded along the wharf Topaz remarked that Mr. Ralph was a real gen'leman. 'He not lak' dat Miss Paula,' she added darkly.

Tina's nerves were suddenly alerted and she wanted to ask Topaz what she was getting at. Joe, her husband, had been on the scene the morning Joanna had died, he had saved John's life and he could have seen something he had later confided to his wife. She felt Topaz looking at her out of the sides of her eyes and firmly bit back the questions that clamoured. Rachel Courtney had warned her not to sift over the dead ashes, to let them blow away, and Tina, spotting a sea fresh display of clawless crabs on the quayside, walked over and began to bargain for some in the patois she was fast learning.

'You're getting to be a real smart housewife, ma'am,' Topaz said admiringly when they were stacking the shopping into the boot of the car. 'Dem crabs got plenty meat in their innards an' taste fine stuffed with rice and onions, then peppered and buttered.'

Tina encouraged kitchen talk on the way home, for Topaz with a touch of the 'mysteries', as she called them, was inclined to plunge her into a mood of introspection that led in the end to the blues. She might again find herself trespassing into the shadows that must always haunt the life she had chosen—for instance, from the ocean side of Blue Water there were a trio of upper windows with sea-blue curtains always drawn across them, and there had been a morning when she had stood gazing at them, evidently noticed by Topaz, who later told her that the apartment had been slept in and used by the first wife of Mr. John.

The challenge to take a look at the rooms had struck through Tina then and there, but she had not gone into them until a few days later, in a blue mood because John remained a charming but distant companion. Passing the rose window on the left curve of the gallery the sun had struck red through the diamond facets, flooding Tina in its ominous glare before she walked under the archway that led into a picture room and thence to the door she was determined to open.

Her fingers shook on the porcelain handle and out had swept a smell of crushed frangipani, once peach-sweet, now bitter and dead. Everything was covered, nothing was dusty, yet the rooms were tomb-like. The thick aquamarine carpet in the boudoir deadened all sound as she walked in. She saw her own colourless reflection in the Adam mirror above the marble fireplace, gilt cupids straddled it in a mischievous manner that was strangely pathetic now there was no lovely woman to gaze in the mirror, touch a hand to dark red hair and hear beyond the window the flurry of the incoming tide.

The pale bedroom furniture embellished with giltwork was also covered in dust sheets which Tina flipped back for a moment. The bed was stripped . . . a great swan bed drifting through a sea of carpet that again was the colour of the eyes Joanna had worshipped. Here the bitter, dead frangipani scent was even stronger, acid, like a crushed peach stone. Tina stared at the long, built-in clothing closets, then impelled as though by a hand she slid them open. Gone were the silks, the chiffon and the organza in which Joanna would have looked like a dream. Gone the glistening furs, the tiny shoes, the yachting outfits. Gone the woman, but not the ghost! Tina hurried away, but for hours afterwards the scent of dead frangipani was in her nostrils.

Did John ever go into Joanna's rooms, there to touch the elegant furniture she had chosen and which would have blended so perfectly with her loveliness? Did he stand at the windows and listen to the sea and hear in it the sound of a voice? A voice that sobbingly asked him why he had ceased to care?

*   *   *

The Carrish bungalow turned out to be large and picturesque, set in a fringe of flame trees and palms so that it was provided with an air of privacy. The roof was of curly green tiles, the stucco walls a fresh cream, while a gaily-striped canopy covered the sun-following veranda. There was a neat front garden with symmetrical paths between carefully tended beds of flowers . . . no friendly, lolloping dog here to bury its bones under the peach trees and tread dirt into the lounge.

'Haven't you a pet, Ralph?' Tina asked, more for something to say than because she thought it likely. Paula didn't look the sort who liked animals around.

'Over at the plantation we have a couple of guard dogs,' he smiled, taking in Tina's slender figure in a blue two-piece, her hair held back in a matching butterfly bow at the nape of her neck. 'You look very cool and pretty,' he added admiringly.

'Why, thank you.' She smiled back at him and thought what a pity it was that he was unattached. He was too nice not to havc a girl of his own to whom hc could give affection.

'Shall we have a drink before I show you over the plantation?' he asked.

She nodded and sat down on the settee of jade-green velvet that stretched along one wall. Beside it there was a coffee table illumined, in the evenings, by a hanging lamp of opaque glass. The cane chairs flared like fans on slender black legs, cushioned in emerald and orange, and Ralph stood mixing drinks at a cocktail bar that had a frame plaited from cane and a glass counter. The room echoed Paula's personality in every detail, especially so in the ebony voodoo masks on the pale green walls and the great spray of some waxen-looking plant in a copper container that was almost the colour of her rich, glossy hair.

Ralph brought a tulip-shaped tumbler to Tina, in which there was a dash of gin over cracked ice, fresh lime halves squeezed of their juice, then tonic almost to the silvered rim. 'Cheers!' he said, sitting down beside her and hoisting one long leg over the other.

'Mmm,' she sipped and wrinkled an appreciative nose, 'you mix a tasty gin-sling.'

'How's John?' he asked. 'I haven't seen

anything of him for a couple of weeks. I suppose,' with a grin, 'he's still in the honeymoon throes.'

'He's busily at work on a new project,' she said, her nose in her drink and a coral flush tingling the tips of her cheekbones. 'Does he leave the entire running of the plantation to you, Ralph?'

'Sure, but I don't mind. John's the artistic type and you can't expect him to get enthusiastic about keeping banana trees free of pest and whether or not the yearly crop of lemons is worth the trouble of growing them. Our oranges are great, nothing there to grumble about, but I pull out my hair over the lemons.' He touched a wry hand to a thinning temple. 'Don't like to be beaten, that's the trouble!'

'No one likes to be beaten,' she smiled wistfully, giving more away by the quality of that smile than she had intended. She saw a keenness come into Ralph's eyes and she edged her glance away from his until it was resting on that dramatic display of waxen flowers. The flesh of the flowers was Paula's, the gloss of the container held the hidden fires of her strange deep nature . . .

'As an old friend of John's and someone who cares about his happiness, may I ask you a question, Tina?' Ralph asked quietly.

She cradled her drink for a pulsing moment, then looked at him. 'Go ahead, Ralph,' she tried to speak lightly. 'I suppose you want to know if we're hitting it off?'

'Please,' he touched her wrist, 'don't think me a Paul Pry, but there are people to whom happiness doesn't come easily. John is one of them, my sister another—you may be a third.'

'You—make us sound quite a triangle.' A jab of pain made her speak sharply. 'D-does it show so plainly that I'm not living in a bridal seventh-heaven?'

'There's no such thing,' he said deliberately. 'You're wise enough to know that what makes a marriage is a sound, down-to-earth relationship based on a foundation of mutual trust, respect, allied aims and physical compatibility. You're what John needs, what he's never had—' Ralph's fingers made a hard bracelet about her wrist. 'Do you throw up defences against him? Defences you aren't consciously aware of? Like me you're an introvert, and I know what it feels like to dread opening up and getting hurt.'

Oh, God, how right he was! How fearful

the dread of a cool stare in answer to a warm confession of love! 'He doesn't love me—can you blame me for guarding my heart?' she whispered, her throat thick with pain.

'What makes you so sure about the state of his heart?' Ralph pressed.

Her eyes widened and filled with the anguish of remembering the devils she had let loose in John when she had taunted him for marrying her instead of Paula. 'You should know,' the words broke from her, 'you're Paula's brother!'

'Ah!' Sudden lines of pain etched Ralph's face and he looked very much his age. He gulped his drink, set aside the tumbler and sat forward with his gaze moodily fixed upon the polished logwood floor. Outside in the garden a bird squawked and Tina saw the muscles tauten under Ralph's white shirt as though the sound jarred on the nerves she had exposed. 'Does it help,' he murmured, 'if I say that I'm sure John never loved my sister? That what was between them—'

'Please,' Tina got feverishly to her feet, 'let's not talk about it any more! Show me round the plantation—come on!' She held out a hand to him and he took it, firmly, and they went out into the sunshine and made their way among the palms and the flame trees towards the tangy scent of citrus fruits that hung thick on the warm air. In a fever of interest, Tina insisted on seeing everything—the nursery where the oranges and tangerines were cultivated, the jagged banana forest where the great hands of fruit glinted amber here, deep green there. She was shown round the big processing plant and the packing sheds, filled with the sing-song chatter of the coloured workers. It was strange and unreal that she was the 'missus' to all these people, that they fell silent and shy when she drew near because the owner of all this was her husband.

Almost two hours later, wilting from the heat, Tina returned to the bungalow with Ralph—and there in the lounge, a moon-pale curve on the velvet settee, was Paula in a stunning dress of white crepe. Seated nearby in a cane chair was a large figure with corn-gold hair, the aromatic smoke of a thin Havana drifting about him. He loomed to his feet as Tina appeared, and dreadfully conscious of Paula, she stammered a greeting in reply to Dacier's: 'How nice that we meet again, Mrs. Trecarrel!

'Hullo, Mr. D'Andremont,' she murmured.

'Don't glower at me, Ralph,' Paula drawled at her brother, who wore a frown as he stepped into the room. 'I developed a bad head at the water-polo match, so Dacier brought me home. I know it's inconvenient, but you've had enough sandwiches and canapés made for an extra guest.'

'Sorry you've a headache,' Ralph growled, nodding hullo at the whimsically smiling Frenchman. 'Naturally there are enough eats to go round. Tina, please sit down.'

She did so, her legs woolly and her pulse already accelerated by that energetic tour of the plantation. Paula was looking across at her, indolent and exotic there against the flattering velvet, her hair in a glistening swathe to one shoulder. Her dress had a neck-plunge which shafted well down between her model's breasts, and Tina felt sure than in contrast to Paula she must look immature and prim.

'Dahling,' the other woman said to her, 'are you going to return Ralph's hospitality by inviting us to dinner one evening?'

'Polly—'

'Oh, hush up, Ralph,' she said to him. 'Tina's out of honeymoon purdah now, and I want Dacier to meet John. Well, what about it, Tina?'

'I—I'd certainly like all three of you to come to dinner one evening,' Tina stammered. 'I'll arrange it.'

'There's a nice little thing,' Paula purred, stretching a pale arm along the top of the settee and digging her long nails into the velvet—just as a cat does when excited. 'Now let's have tea brought in, Ralph. My head suddenly feels a lot better.'

Ralph stared hard at his sister, then as he swung towards the door Tina saw that his lips were compressed, his nostrils white-edged. It could have been with anger—or was it the tormenting love that bound him as to an unpredictable, dangerous child?

CHAPTER EIGHT

TINA told John at breakfast that she was thinking of giving a small dinner-party. He quirked a smile across the table and told her it was okay with him. 'Who's coming?' he wanted to know.

'Ralph and Paula,' she replied, dabbing at her lips with a napkin to hide the nerve that flickered at the thought of having Paula here, near John. 'Dacier d'Andremont is also coming, and I wondered if you could suggest a nice local girl I could invite as a partner for Ralph.'

'There's Janet Macrae,' John said, adding in a provocative tone of voice, 'She's only about nineteen, but we greying males rather like them dewy with innocence.'

A brief meeting of eyes followed this crack, and Tina, nerves rippling under her rib-cage, wondered what he would do if she suddenly went round to him and kissed that glistening speck of marmalade off his bottom lip. 'Yes, Janet should be perfect,' she agreed, having met and liked the older Macrae girl when she and John had collected Liza the morning after the younger girl's birthday party. Janet was sandy-haired and healthy-looking, with an open kind of personality that would surely make a relaxing change for Ralph, who was continually in the company of the sphinx-like Paula . . .

'Getting matchmaking ideas with regard to Ralph?' John inquired, elbows on the table, cleft chin propped on his knuckles, sea-blue eyes regarding her with amusement.

'He's extremely nice,' she smiled back. 'He works like a Trojan for you, and I must admit that I think he'd make the right sort of girl a charming husband.'

'And where does Paula fit into the cosy domestic picture you're painting?' The smile had died out of John's eyes and now they were almost hard. 'Do you think this rich landowner is planning to take her back with him to Martinique?'

John's taut expression drove a knife-point into Tina's heart, and she wished passionately that Dacier was romantically interested in Paula, but she didn't think it likely. Though the pair of them seemed to enjoy crossing swords, once or twice yesterday Tina had noticed him looking at Paula with a cold, almost repelled look in his amber eyes. No, she wasn't the type of woman Dacier went for. When he had said he thought it likely he would one day lose his heart to an English girl—it was true Paula had been born in England—there was a Continental provocation about her that made her the *femme fatale* type Dacier had not been referring to.

After breakfast, when John had gone to

his studio, Tina changed into a bathing suit and went down to the beach. The tide was out, so wearing grass sandals she waded towards the reef where there was a fascinating underwater galaxy of rainbow-tinted fish and fretted coral. She splashed about like a child, letting the tiny fish swim between her fingers, fairy things with wings you could see through. The coral grew like tree ferns and caverns, making a weird fable-like world where loggerhead turtles paddled along, encrusted with barnacles, and orange starfish lay like plump pincushions on sandy patches between the yellow coral rocks. What she had to watch for was the black sea-urchins, whose spikes were both painful and poisonous, and what she most delighted in were the cobalt-blue fish no larger than a thumbnail.

At last, replete with all this strange beauty, she returned to the beach with her hair in wet tendrils and stretched out on her orange and white striped beach-jacket. The sea-carved cliffs rose all around her like a shell, holding her enclosed in the hollow booming of the sea, its eternal motion rocking her off to sleep.

She awoke drowsily, unaware that

someone was sprawled nearby watching her. Indolent from the sun, she stretched her young body in its white swimwear; her legs were slender and pale-gold, the left knee resting against the bend of her slightly updrawn right leg, her fingers digging the sand in surprise when a voice said: 'You are a pocket Venus, *ma belle*.'

She swung her glance to the right, and there was Dacier d'Andremont, large and strikingly attractive in fawn slacks and a bamboo-gold shirt. His smile flashed and as he quickly sat up, a plump peach landed in her lap. 'I find them most refreshing, don't you?' His white teeth sank into one, and the sweet, slightly acid fragrance drifted to Tina's nostrils and made them quiver.

Again, as Tina nibbled the juicy peach and knuckled the moisture from her chin, she was aware of being with someone who was totally sympathetic and dependable—and yet he didn't actually look it. With his lionesque head, those whimsical eyes, that vitality-packed frame, she felt herself with a man who knew a tremendous lot about women. The nice thing was, he didn't exploit his knowledge but charmingly pretended that he could still be fooled.

'Did you come to Blue Water on purpose

to see me?' she asked.

'I did.' He rested on an elbow and prodded his peach stone into the pale sand. 'It was that yesterday you looked a little sad, *mignonne*. Has your good husband already lost interest in his bride?'

She scrubbed her fingers hard on her beach-jacket and felt a flush prickle her skin. 'That's a leading question, Mr. d'Andremont, one I could take exception to. After all, this is only the third time we have met.'

'Once is often enough for two people to establish that they are in sympathy with each other.' He dug a hand into a back pocket and produced his opulent cigarette case. 'You do not smoke, I think?'

She shook her head. 'I'm the old-fashioned type,' she said wryly.

'Don't be on the defensive about that—Tina.' He glanced over the flame of his lighter, then snapped it out. 'I may call you by your cute first name, no?'

'Go ahead,' she smiled, wondering a little if he was flirting with her. Very rarely had she been flirted with. John had courted her in a curiously matter-of-fact way—probably because the urge to fall in love was dead in him.

'What are you thinking, Tina?' Dacier puffed the smoke of a Gauloise. 'That a French bachelor should not call a married woman a pocket Venus, that he must pretend he much prefers to look at, say, that palm tree over there?'

'I think palm trees are very graceful things,' she fenced, flipping a narrow chiffon scarf out of her beach-jacket pocket and preparing to tie back her hair with it. The next moment Dacier had calmly plucked it out of her fingers and dropped it to the sand like a ruby cloud.

'Leave your hair as it is,' he ordered. 'Beautiful things should not be tamed and tied.'

'Oh, come off it, Dacier!' she laughed. 'It's good of you to want to boost my morale, but don't overdo it.'

'So,' he shrugged his shoulders in an amusing Latin way, 'my compliments are wasted on the wife of John Trecarrel. What, then, shall we talk about? Marriage?'

'It's always an interesting subject,' she agreed, arms clasped about her updrawn knees, her gaze upon the shifting silver of the ocean.

'Interesting and complex,' he

murmured. 'Especially so when a girl loses her heart to a much older man who has already been married. It takes courage, that.'

She looked at him, aware that he was genuinely concerned for her and not probing just to satisfy curiosity. 'Yes, I have a concern for you,' he nodded. 'You are a sincere, warm-hearted girl with, I think, the capacity for much devotion. Had we met when you were free I frankly tell you that I should have laid siege to your affections ... ah, you laugh again and think I make the joke!'

'I do indeed think you make the joke,' she retorted, looking at him and taking in the facial lines which the sun revealed, the hint of self-indulgence about his bold mouth. 'I bet you've laid siege to quite a few female hearts in your time.'

'Women are as a man finds them,' he admitted shamelessly. 'The fruit for the plucking is plucked. The shy, green kind is left alone until a man feels he needs or wants a wife.'

'And in that way you men reap the best of both worlds,' Tina shot back. 'Mother Nature certainly favours your sex, doesn't she?'

'She is a female,' he chuckled, drawing on his cigarette with an arrogant movement of his blond head. 'Come, wouldn't life be a lot less exciting if men were tame creatures to be led about by the nose? Would *you* want that? I think not, for you are far too feminine. It is those with too many aggressive hormones who desire to wear the pants. Ugh, such women I do not like!'

'Have you known many?' she grinned.

'Not at Martinique, nor in Paris. But America and England have their quota. Marriage with such a one *I* would not like.'

'You want to be the boss, of course.'

'I will allow her a little temperament,' he smiled. 'The aiming of a vase or a teapot, you understand.'

'Oh, do Frenchmen recommend that as a marriage stabilizer?'

'We admit that living in close community with another human being is the most provocative situation on earth—ah, I see from the widening of your eyes that you agree—and all sorts of tensions arise. Think of the relief it brings to aim something, therefore, knowing women to be notoriously bad aimers, it should be a fairly safe way of allowing one's wife to let off steam.'

'The solutions to marital problems always seem simple until we're up against them,' Tina said, filtering sand through her fingers and losing her smile.

'What is your especial problem, Tina?' Dacier asked gently. 'Would it help to discuss it?'

'I—don't know,' she shrugged. 'Aiming china at John wouldn't solve it, that's for sure.'

Dacier swept a glance over her pensive face, then stubbing his cigarette in the sand, he said: 'We have been acquainted a very short while, but each of us knows that already we have established a feeling of understanding, therefore as a friend I am going to speak candidly. You are not happy in your marriage, is it not so? You find yourself part of a situation which bewilders and unnerves you—and I do not like to see this. You said, when first we met, that your husband was haunted by the past. The ghosts, they are still there, up in the house above the beach? They hover between you and John Trecarrel?'

She shivered at the graphic way he put it, and the need for his sympathy gripped her and would not be denied. 'I thought I could help John to forget,' she said, 'but it needed love—his love for me. Instead there's a wall between us. We smile at each other, we discuss daily matters, but we feel the barrier whenever we touch . . .'

Her lashes clung in sudden wet points, young and hurt was her look, while her pale, untied hair swung to conceal the tears she fought to control. She felt Dacier take hold of her hands and firmly press them. She heard him say: 'A marriage that gives sadness and little joy is not for you, *chérie*. A one-sided love holds the seeds of disaster, and when they are fully sown it is you who will reap the bitter harvest—'

'Oh, don't!' Tina put her head against her knees as though in physical pain, for there was too much truth in what he said for it to be bearable. She had cocooned herself in a padding of hope and desperate activity for the past couple of weeks, now Dacier had bared her aching heart and her unloved body, and she was afraid and quivering as a moth that must fly or die. His fingers cupped her chin and he made her look at him. His pupils were enlarged darkly against the amber irises of his eyes and she stared into them, then his hands slipped to her shoulders and he was suddenly leaning so close that she felt the warmth coming off his tanned skin. She was held motionless, desperately aware of her hungry need for tenderness.

'There are no ghosts in my past, Tina,' he murmured. 'My heart would like to be filled with you—only you.'

What was he saying? What was he doing? She came alive to the fact that he had eased her back on to her beach-jacket and that his wide, brown shoulders were blocking the sun, that for seconds on end had she lain like this, aware of him, and yet unaware that it was as a lover that he was speaking and acting.

'No,' her hands pressed against his shoulders and she fought him off, 'you mustn't, Dacier!' She scrambled clear of him, snatched up her jacket and fled to the steps that led upwards and home. She had mounted about five of them, when, thrusting back her tumbling hair, she saw someone confronting her—lean, grim-faced, carved in stone against the wild frangipani that cascaded down the cliff wall.

'John!' She gazed at him in stunned horror, immediately realizing that from here he would have looked down upon Dacier's broad back as he leant over her own passive figure. It could only have looked like a love scene!

'Aren't you going to invite the boy-friend for lunch? he crisped, his eyes like blue stones in that dark mask of a face. 'I mean, let's extend to him the hospitality of the dining-room as well.'

Tina, too stricken for speech, heard a crunch behind her as Dacier mounted the steps. 'You must not misconstrue what you have just seen, Trecarrel,' he said. 'We were talking, nothing more.'

'The indications were that it was an absorbing—conversation.' John had never looked more savage and biting, and as he swept a look of sheer contempt over Tina, she shrank for instinctive protection against Dacier's bulk—an action that triggered John to further sarcasm. 'If the pair of you must indulge in clandestine thrills, then you'd better do it where I or my servants are not likely to overlook the proceedings. Or has the affair reached a stage where the pair of you are beyond controlling your feelings?'

'John—how dare you say that!' Tina gasped, violated by the conclusion to which he had jumped. 'I won't be accused in this way—it's uncalled-for!'

'My dear,' he leant forward with glittering eyes, 'even with your husband you don't get sociable in such a relaxed position . . . my God, it's the reverse, isn't it?'

His scorn lashed, and like a small animal driven by sheer pain she clawed him in return. 'Not all of us want love affairs with other people, so don't go judging me by your own standards,' she retorted.

He stared, bitterly, straight down into her eyes. The blood drained away from under his tan and his face had a carved, livid look, then he swung on his heel and leapt up the steps, stumbling once as though his left leg almost let him down. Tina gave a small cry, unaware, when she saw that, then he had gone and she was turning anguished eyes to Dacier.

'I—I never meant to say that to him,' she whispered.

Dacier gripped her elbows with large, warm hands. 'Poor little one, what can I say to help you? This man with the scarred heart that still bleeds is the one you love, eh?'

'I wonder if it can be love?' she sighed. 'It feels more like hell on earth.'

'Tina,' his fingers tightened on her arms,

‘is this marriage not a normal one? You understand that it can be annulled if that is the case.’

‘I know.’ She spoke tiredly and wished to be alone with her wounds and her regrets. It was all over now, this strange dream of happiness at which she had clutched as one does a drifting leaf in the fall, holding it tight, wishing with all youth’s ardour, only to find it crumbling to brittle little pieces. ‘Yes, I know, Dacier. I daresay that will happen now.’

He said no more until they reached the headland, holding her hand and helping her to mount the wide steps. Then they stood outlined against the clear blue sky, a man and a girl in all their promising youth who might have looked like sweethearts to a casual observer. The trade wind blew the fine strands of hair in a loop about Tina’s neck, and as she disentangled them she remembered so clearly another headland above a sea that was not a burning sapphire. She remembered a long shadow falling across the windswept grass and a voice saying: ‘Stand just as you are, gazing out to sea as though the realization of a dream awaits you on the other side of the horizon . . .’

She shivered, and Dacier must have thought she was looking ahead in trepidation. Strangely enough there was no fear in her, only a defeated hopelessness, a void, a feeling that the inevitable had come to pass.

'Come with me, now,' Dacier said, his fingers warm over the breakable bones of her shoulders. 'It is plain from what I have just seen of John Trecarrel that he's a man with a fierce temper, and I feel afraid for you, *mignonne*.'

Tina's eyes clung to Dacier's, a catch in her throat when she recalled John's passionate loss of control the evening he had bruised her with his lips and his hands. She had thought then that he was furious enough to kill her, yet with that loyalty which is part of feminine love she said, lightly: 'Oh, I don't suppose he'll beat me.'

'I was not thinking of a—beating, *ma chère*.' Dacier's deep, gay voice was changed and ominous, while a cloud rolled over the face of the sun and the brightness died for a long moment, like a wiped out smile.

'You're referring to John's first wife, aren't you, Dacier?' Tina spoke sharply. 'It's true she died in strange circumstances, but John wasn't—he wasn't entirely to blame for that—I suppose you've been listening to Paula's distorted side of the story?'

'Paula talks, I listen, but I draw my own conclusions,' he replied quietly. 'I would say that Joanna deliberately sought death and that it was hushed up by friends of the Trecarrels.'

'John almost died himself, did Paula tell you that?' Tina was husky with emotion, and as the sun blossomed hotly again it was as though she stood in a flood of revelation. Words re-echoed in her mind, John demanding of her, their first night at Blue Water, that she give him peace, not nagging suspicion about other women. Ralph insinuating that Joanna was possessive to the point where it was no longer normal. Rachel Courtney backed up this statement on the cay when she had said that Joanna seemed helplessly appealing ... and unable to share a man with his work.

Joanna hadn't wanted to share John with anything ... anyone ... at any time. She had made his life such a hell of suspicion and demands that Paula's silky, mocking provocation would have drawn him like a magnet. But it hadn't been love which he had felt for her. It had been a man, as he had thought, with an adult woman.

'The Carrish cousins possessed my husband and tore him down the middle, like tigresses!' Tina gasped. She shot an anguished glance towards Blue Water House, whose great roof showed through the trees of the garden. She wanted to run to John, to give him all that he hadn't found before in his search for love . . .

'You want to dash again like a—a moth into flame,' Dacier murmured whimsically. 'And that is love, eh, a pain we cannot keep away from.' His hands slipped from her shoulders. 'Go to him, *mignonne*, try to remedy the damage. If you need—a friend, I shall be waiting at my hotel.'

'Thank you, Dacier.' She smiled at him, then swung her beach-jacket over her shoulder, the touchingly jaunty action of a soldier going into action. 'I'll be seeing you.'

She walked away from him, the big man who might have loved her without ever hurting her, along the path that led to John. Her heart had little hope to feed on, but she loved him and she was going to tell him so. If, after that, he still wished her to go, she would set her teeth and go.

She entered the fan-cooled hall of the house and ran upstairs to her room. She stood still a moment, listening for a movement from John's room, but everything was strangely webbed in silence. Hot and sticky from the beach, she took a quick tepid shower, then slipped into a lightly pleated cream silk dress. She brushed her hair and French-pleated it, then put on a dash of lipstick, for there was little colour under her light honey tan. The enormity of separation from John might be gaping ahead of her, yet she had to force herself to calmness and go downstairs. The rosewood clock chimed as she walked past it, silvery in the quietness, and she breathed the scent of the syringa she had arranged yesterday in an antique vase on the hall table. She was conscious again of the waiting stillness in possession of the house, and with her hand on the knob of the dining-room door, she stole a glance at the splendidly carved double staircase—did someone watch unseen from that pool of ruby on the landing, lips already curved in a smile of victory?

Tina's skin prickled clammily, and apprehension quickened in her when she entered the dining-room. It was empty, and there was only one place laid for lunch!

She pressed the service-bell and when Nathaniel came in she almost wept with relief at seeing his seamed face and familiar grey-haired dignity. The house, after all, hadn't been taken over by ghosts!

In his soft, polite voice the old manservant told her that Mr. John had gone somewhere in his car about half an hour ago. 'He say not to lay his place for lunch, ma'am.'

'All right, Nathaniel.' She managed a smile. 'I'll make do with salad and not bother with dessert.'

He withdrew from the room and quietly closed the door, leaving her alone to pick at the food on her plate, the honey-panelled room loud with questions. Coffee was brought to her and she drank it too hot and too quickly, little snakes of perspiration trickling down her back as she paced about, unable to relax, her heart like lead in her breast.

She kept thinking of Paula Carrish, deadly certain that if she were to go to the phone in the hall and dial Ralph's number, he would confirm the horrible suspicion that John had gone to the plantation, that he was with Paula, the woman to whom he had turned before!

Tina's hands came together in unconscious supplication and she found herself crossing the hall to the staircase. She mounted to the gallery and came awake like a sleepwalker outside the door of John's studio. She turned the handle and felt the cool air of the room waft against her skin, saw the pallid sculptures with their secret eyes, breathed the moist clay mingling with the nutty fragrance of pipe tobacco.

She left the door ajar behind her and moved over to his work bench, where she touched the tools he had been handling that morning. Her fingers crept to the damp edges of the cloth draping the figure he had been working on since their return from Barbados. He had not told her whether it was a man or a woman, and whenever she had probed he had smiled and told her she must await the final unveiling.

She might not be here for that, and, heart thumping, she lifted back the damp muslin and she stared, slow hot tears filling her eyes so that through a wavering mist she gazed at the figure of a girl with windblown hair encircling her slender neck, thin, crane-like limbs, straining forward as though to see over the rim of girlhood into the well of womanhood. It was beautiful, not because *she* was beautiful, but made so by something John had put into it, a poised magic, a quality that transferred a quite ordinary girl into hope, life, promise . . .

'Oh, John!' she whispered, her eyes wet with tears, face to face with the girl John had found and wanted and then lost in the wife who had questioned every kiss, every caress. The girl on the cliff—herself!

But why hadn't he told her? Why hadn't he said . . .

Then with a gasp she swung to face the door, hearing the click of a high heel, breathing a sweet, expensive perfume. A cloud of dark bronze hair framed a cream-skinned face, a thin red mouth slashed the cream, and dark brows winged above jade-green eyes. There was no mistaking that sleek silhouette, and Tina's heart went thump. Paula—here! Had John brought her back with him?

Paula's high heels clicked again on the parquet. She carried a beige bag, her long legs were webbed in sensuous dark nylon, and she wore one of those silk sheaths that suited her so well. It was leaf-green and perfect with her colouring. 'Did I startle you, sweetie?' she drawled. 'You looked at me just now as though I were a ghost who had walked in on you. Well, the door was open and I—' she broke off and her jade eyes settled on John's unfinished sculpture of Tina. There was no mistaking the subject, the features, the limbs and even the pose, which Tina had a way of unconsciously assuming. Youth; unsure, leggy yet graceful, needing so much to be wanted.

'So you've been posing for John?' Paula said.

'N-not exactly. He's working from sketches.'

'It's quite inspired, isn't it? Might turn out to be one of the best pieces he's ever worked on.' Paula stretched a long hand to the figure, so suddenly that her action created a threat, a glint of unholy glee in her eyes as Tina moved quickly to protect the precious thing.

'Leave it alone!' Tina ordered. 'You'll mark it.'

'My, we are touchy,' Paula laughed silkily. 'As though I'd damage anything belonging to John! You don't really think I would, surely?'

'I think you make your own rules, regardless of who gets hurt.' The retort was out of Tina's mouth before she could stop it.

'Really?' The green eyes narrowed. 'You don't like me, do you, Tina? Well, it's mutual; dislike usually is. Whereas love and hate are in bondage to each other. The hairline in between is often so indistinguishable that we're hardly sure whether we're aflame with one or the other. On the other hand there's no mistaking dislike, it's almost a taste in the mouth, and I never had much of a taste for milk and honey. Nor did John, therefore it's no surprise to me that he's brown bored after nibbling your sweet surface and finding only bread underneath.'

Paula studied Tina under painted lashes, the tensing of her body against John's work bench, the way her hands clenched the sides of her dress. 'You were a fool, you know, to marry John. He's years too old for you, past the age for the kisses in the moonlight that stir you young things. Then again—but perhaps I shouldn't be too frank—unless you'd like me to be quite open about things?'

'We might as well let our hair right down,' Tina agreed, feeling herself on the edge of a landslide, reckless of falling, knowing she had been building up false hopes just because John made a sculpture of her. That Paula was here, and obviously aware that Tina and he had quarrelled, was confirmation that he had gone to her and talked and agreed that the women had better clear the air between them, that he was sick and tired of the whole business. That was how he had looked on the beach steps when he had swung away from her, bitter and tired and as though he never wanted to see her again.

The other woman wandered about the studio, touching things, smiling secretly as though she were recalling the occasions when she had modelled for John. She paused in front of a faceless, half-finished Greek sculpture, then she turned and said to Tina: 'You're a novice, a schoolgirl. You've nothing to give a man like John.'

'H-he married me,' Tina fought back.

'Oh, that!' Paula dismissed the absurdity with a sweep of her hand. 'Have you ever heard the Greek legend about there being only one true love for each man and woman? It's true, you know, and all the obstacles in the world won't stop them from coming together in the end.' She stood there looking at Tina, superbly groomed, chiselled out of stone shot through with strange fires. 'You asked for frankness, so I'll be frank, my dear. John loves me, and half a dozen marriages wouldn't ever keep him from me.'

Tina had gone white to her hairline, her lips and nostrils were chalky. 'Why,' she asked, 'did John marry me?'

'Oh, the answer to that is quite simple,' Paula drawled. 'Under that piratical exterior of his, John is a bit of a Puritan. He doesn't like affairs, and he needed a whip to lash my back. He blames me, poor foolish darling, for Joanna's death. Naturally I had nothing to do with it, but for years that suspicion has stood between us. He's hurt me, Tina, in more ways than one, but that's love, isn't it? If we're afraid of getting hurt, we shouldn't play with fire, but how many of us can help grabbing those pretty coals?'

Paula blew on her fingertips, smiled her secret smile, and looked the embodiment of a woman who was close at last to getting what she had always wanted. She looked Tina over, the young body that had grown less angular in the weeks she had been here, the pale skin that was faintly honeyed, the wood-smoke eyes dark in this moment with the pain of shattered hopes. 'You know,' Paula drawled, 'Dacier d'Andremont is quite taken with you, and he's lots richer than John. Why don't you latch on to him?'

'I don't happen to want him,' Tina retorted. 'I love John.'

'Too bad. I've heard he has a fabulous home on Martinique, Bellecombe I think he calls it, and you're much more his type than you ever were John's. Johnny's a complex person; moody, difficult, passionate. Can't you see for yourself that he and I are a pair?'

Tina nodded tiredly. Oh, how tired she was. She wanted to flop across her bed, to weep, to sleep, and then to go. She glanced round the studio in a kind of daze. 'Where is John?' she asked, tears of longing and loss making her speak thickly.

'I'm here, honey,' said his voice, and in through the door he walked. Tina stared at him blindly. No, she couldn't bear any more—she couldn't face both of them and hear it all again, that she was out and Paula was in. She fled to the door, but he stepped in front of her.

'Let me go!' she gasped. 'Paula's told me

everything—there's no more to talk about.'

'I think there is, Tina.' His voice was deep, dark, compelling, and she looked up at him. 'There's quite a lot to talk about, my love.'

My love! She went weak with the shock of it, and then his arm had latched her to his side, tightly, and above her head she heard him say crisply to Paula: 'I've been outside the door listening fascinated to the lying tale you've been spinning this child. It nearly came off a second time, didn't it, but after chatting with Ralph for a while I began to get the oddest feeling that you might have come over here to start on Tina. Maybe it was Ralph's restlessness—the poor guy knows you pretty well, doesn't he? He knows that years ago you lied to Joanna about that crazy friendship I struck up with you, which I've regretted ever since, which was never the love affair you wanted. I didn't love you then, and I don't love you now. Whatever it was that attracted me—well, it died years ago. It died when Jo died.'

Paula, taut as a lance, gazed back at him with the glittering green eyes of a tigress. She was passionate with fury, her scarlet mouth suddenly lashing at him with words of hate—hate, not love.

It went on for minutes, then she swept past them, out of the room, her perfume lingering after her angry footsteps had died away. A tremor ran through Tina, and unaware she had wrapped both arms about John's waist as though to protect him. She heard him laughing very quietly, and when she glanced up at him, he said wryly: 'What a pair we are! Crazy about each other, yet scared stiff to say so in case it wasn't the same for the other person.'

'Is that why you were so angry this morning?' she asked.

'I wanted to knock that guy's handsome head clean off his caveman shoulders.' John swung her to face him and his blue eyes were dark with feeling in his lean face. 'He was bending over you, and there you were, taking it like a lamb, not grabbing a hank of his hair and fighting like a little wildcat . . .'

'Try me now,' she whispered.

And suddenly he was holding her so close and hard that he seemed to want to absorb her into his very being. He was hurting her, but it was a pain she welcomed with all the strength of her love. At last, as surely as she knew the colour of his eyes, she felt the love in him, the passion and the unimaginable need that only she could assuage. She just about managed to say his name, the rest was lost in his kiss.

The length and strength of his kiss—the heaven of it!

'Oh, John!' she gasped, pulling away, burying her face in his shoulder.

'Oh, Tina!' He ruffled her hair, and in a while when she looked at him she saw sparks of fire glimmering in his eyes. A tense awareness vibrated between them, high-voltaged, unbearable, and with a low groan he swung her up into his arms and marched downstairs with her. They saw Nathaniel in the hall, and John, without a touch of embarrassment at being caught carrying his wife, asked that coffee and snacks be brought to them in the salon.

'Yes, sir!' Nathaniel was beaming as he came across to open the doors of the salon. He evidently considered it quite in order for the master of the house to behave in this ardent fashion.

The world closed out and coffee on a table in front of them, they talked at last of Joanna. 'I loved her in the beginning,' he said. 'She was utterly beautiful, like a dream come true, a dream that shattered when I awoke to the reality of her. Love is a gift, not a possession. You give it, you don't take—take. She couldn't help what she was—there's a name for it—and I'm glad the torment didn't go on for her.'

He sat quiet a moment, gripping Tina's hand. 'I guess Liza will be okay. I think she takes after me.'

'She's you all over again, John,' Tina assured him gently.

He nodded and sat looking into Tina's eyes. 'I love you unbearably, do you know that? It hurt like the devil that night you rejected me. I thought you couldn't bear me to touch you.'

'I can bear that,' she said, bringing his hand to her cheek. 'What I couldn't bear was thinking you were making a substitute of me.'

'For Paula?' His hand went round, into her hair, finding the nape of her neck. He drew her forward until her lips were almost under his. 'We're leaving Ste. Monique and our friend Paula. I'm selling Blue Water House and we're going to live at Barbados. We'll be near Liza, and we'll have moonflowers in our garden.'

'When did you decide to do that?' she whispered, weak as water at his closeness, his touch, the love in his eyes.

'After seeing you on the beach with d'Andremont. I drove off in a temper, then I decided that this damn place was unlucky for us and I stopped off to see Ralph and to ask his advice. He agreed that it might be a good plan to get shot of the house, for us to get away together. Is it a good plan, my darling?'

'A lovely plan.' Her voice died, but everything else was gloriously alive as he lifted her completely into his arms and started to make up for some of the time they had lost. When Tina could get her breath a little, she held him away with her fingers at his dented chin. 'Before we go any further,' she begged, 'let me apologize for that mean thing I said to you on the beach steps this morning. I—didn't really mean it.'

'You meant every word, you little fibber,' but he was smiling as he spoke, tender and gay, years wiped away from him, 'and it's going to take more than an apology to get round me.'

'What have I got to do?' The tips of her fingers no longer tingled in vain for that dent in his chin.

'I'll think of something,' he promised,

brushing at the fair hair he had tumbled with his kisses. 'Life's going to be good from now on, eh? We'll make out together.'

'I'm sure of it, John.' She pressed her cheek to his and hugged him with tight, loving arms. How she had wanted this, to be absolutely certain of his love for her, and his need for her. Yes, life was going to be good with this man of hers who was no longer a stranger who held aloof because he was unsure of *her*.

Photoset, printed and bound in Great Britain by
REDWOOD BURN LIMITED, Trowbridge, Wiltshire